For Émile and Germaine,
Alice and Henri, Louis and Simone / the roots.
For Samuel, Antoine and Cécile / the fruits.

MARIE-SABINE ROGER

SOFT IN
THE HEAD

Translated from the French
by Frank Wynne

PUSHKIN PRESS
LONDON

Pushkin Press
71–75 Shelton Street,
London WC2H 9JQ

Original text © Editions du Rouergue, 2008
Translation © Frank Wynne 2016
First published in French as *La Tête en friche* in 2008
This translation first published by Pushkin Press in 2016

1 3 5 7 9 8 6 4 2

ISBN 978 1 782271 58 1

Set in Monotype Baskerville by Tetragon, London
Printed in Great Britain by the CPI Group, UK

www.pushkinpress.com

I 'VE DECIDED to adopt Margueritte. She'll be eighty-six any day now so there seemed no point putting it off. Old people have a tendency to die.

This way, if something happened to her, like, I don't know, say she had a fall in the street, I'd be there. I'd show up, elbow my way through the crowd and say:

"OK, that's enough, you can all bugger off now. I'll take care of everything, she's my grandmother."

It's not like she'd be wearing a sign saying she was only adopted.

I'll be able to buy a newspaper and a packet of mints for her. I'll be able to sit next to her in the park, visit her at Les Peupliers on Sundays. Even stay for lunch if I feel like it.

Obviously, I could have done all this stuff before now, but I'd have felt like I was just a hanger-on. In the future, I'll do it gladly but also out of a sense of responsibility. That's the real difference: I'll have family responsibilities. That's something I figure I'll be good at.

It's changed my life, meeting her, meeting Margueritte. It's weird having someone to worry about when I'm alone—someone other than myself I mean. I'm not used to it. I never had any family before her.

Well, you know what I mean. Obviously, I've got a mother, goes without saying. Thing is that, apart from being lumbered with each other for nine months, me and her had nothing in common except bad times. If there were good times, I don't remember any. And obviously I had a father. Not that I had him around for long, he did his thing with my mother and skedaddled. That said, it didn't stop me growing up bigger and stronger than the average kid: 110 kilos of muscle, not a gram of fat, a metre eighty-nine in socks and built to match. If my parents had wanted me, I would have been their pride and joy. No such luck.

The other thing that's new for me is that before Margueritte, I'd never loved another person. I'm not talking about sex stuff, I'm talking about the sort of feeling where you don't end up in bed after. Tenderness and affection, and trust. All those things. I still have trouble saying the actual words since no one ever said them to me until Margueritte brought it up. Feelings that are decent and pure.

I want to make that clear, because I know people who would be dumb enough to say, hey, Germain, are you hitting on grannies these days? Copping off with OAPs?

The sort of people I'd happily give a smack in the mouth.

It's a pity I didn't know Margueritte when I would have got some mileage out of her, back when I was a kid, when I was into all sorts of devilment.

But there's no point regretting things in this life: what's past is behind us.

I'm a self-made man, built myself from the ground up. OK, maybe I didn't follow the proper building regulations, but I'm still standing.

Margueritte on the other hand is shrinking. She hunches when she sits, bent over her knees. I'll have to take good care of her if she's going to last. She makes out she's tough as old boots when really she's fragile. She's got the bones of a sparrow, I could snap them between two fingers easy. I'm just saying. Obviously I wouldn't do it. People don't go round breaking their grandmother's bones, that would be sick. It's just my way of explaining how frail she is. She reminds me of the spun glass figurines they sell at Granjean's newsagents. Especially the little doe in the window. It's tiny, with thin, wiry legs. No thicker than an eyelash. Margueritte is like that. Every time I walk past and see that doe, I think about buying it. Three euros, it's not much, is it? But I know the minute I put it in my pocket it would break. And besides, where would I keep it? There's not much in the way of shelves at my place. Caravans don't have much space.

It was the same with Margueritte at first, I just didn't have the room. I mean inside me. When I started to feel feelings I realized I'd have to make space for her and for my feelings. Because loving her came on top of everything else—all the stuff already cluttering up my head—and I hadn't planned for it. So I did some clearing out. It made me realize there wasn't much there I wanted to keep hold of. My head was a jumble of stupid rubbish. TV game shows, radio phone-ins, conversations with Jojo Zekouc at Chez Francine café-restaurant. Playing a couple of hands of belote with Marco, Julien and Landremont. And then there were the nights I went round to see Annette to dip my wick and be all lovey-dovey. But that's good for the brain, actually, because you can't think when you've got blue balls. Or not properly, anyway, not deeply.

I'll tell you about Annette another time. Things are different now between Annette and me.

T HE FIRST TIME I saw Margueritte, she was sitting on that bench over there. Under the big linden tree next to the pond. It was about three in the afternoon, the sun was shining and the weather was much too warm for the season. It's not good for the trees: they start budding like nobody's business and then if there's a cold snap, all the flowers die off and there's not much fruit.

She was dressed the same as always. Obviously, that first day I couldn't know that she always dressed like that. You only find out other people's habits when you get to know them. The first time you meet, you can't know what's going to happen. You don't know if maybe you'll fall in love. If you'll even remember the first time later on. Or maybe you'll end up screaming abuse and pissing each other off. Or maybe you'll just become friends. With all the *ifs* and *ors* that go with it.

The *maybes* are the worst.

Margueritte was sitting there, doing nothing, staring into space. She was facing the lawn and the far end of the main path. She was wearing a print dress with grey and purple flowers the same colour as her hair, a tightly buttoned grey jacket and dark stockings and shoes. Next to her on the bench was a black handbag.

I couldn't help thinking she was being careless. Leaving her handbag like that, I could nick it any time I wanted.

When I say *I*, *I* doesn't mean me personally. *I* in this case stands for *people in general*. Well, chavs, anyway. Especially since she's a little old lady, doing a runner would be a piece of piss. You just push her with the flat of your hand, a quick shove would be enough: she falls down with a little yelp, fractures her hip and lies there half dead while you—obviously I don't mean you or me personally—you make a quick getaway, simple as, in fact by now you'd already be long gone. Don't ask me how I know this stuff. Look, all I'm saying is that she wasn't being careful.

I might just as easily not have been to the park the Monday I met her. I might have been busy, I might have been up to my eyes. What do you think I do with my time? Some days I've got things I have to do: measuring the trunks of the fir trees along the bypass using my hands to check for deforestation. (Half of them are going to die, I'm sure they are, that's why I check. It's hardly surprising they die when you see the botched job the guys from the municipal parks committee make of the planting.) Training to run for as long as possible, shooting tin cans with an airgun outside the caravan. It's all about breathing and reflexes, I need to be ready in case I'm ever caught up in a terrorist attack, or if I have to save people or something. And there's a bunch of other things. Different stuff. For example, I whittle bits of wood with my Opinel penknife. I carve animals and little figurines. People I see in the street, cats, dogs, anything and anyone.

Other days I go to the park to count the pigeons.

On the way, I write my name in capital letters on the marble plaque underneath the soldier on the war memorial. Obviously, every time I do, someone they send from the council cleans it off and gives me a bollocking. You have to stop with this shit, Germain, we've had enough—next time you'll have to clean it off yourself!

I wouldn't mind but the markers are supposed to be indelible—*impossible to efface or erase; see also: inerasable*—and they cost me quite a bit. In fact, I'm going to tell them down at the stationery shop that this is false advertising. The pack was clearly marked "for all surfaces", I've been gypped. Marble is a surface—unless I'm very much mistaken, as Margueritte always says.

Anyway, as soon as my name has been erased, I've got no choice but to start over again. It doesn't matter to me, I'm a patient man. If I keep going, they might end up leaving it.

Besides, I can't see where the harm is, my name's right down at the bottom. It's not even in alphabetical order, and I could kick up a fuss because Chazes doesn't come at the end, far from it. By rights I should be fifth on their list.

Between Pierre Boisverte and Ernest Combereau.

One day I said this to Jacques Devallée down at the town hall, he's a civil serpent. He nodded, he said that basically I was right, that lists of names are made to have other names added.

Though it has to be said that he added: But there's something you need to bear in mind...

"Oh, what's that?" I said, all casual.

13

"Well, if you look carefully, you'll notice that all the people whose names are engraved on the memorial have one thing in common: they're dead."

"Oh, right!" I said, "I see, so that's how it is. So to be on the list you have to kick the bucket?"

"That is, in effect, about the size of it, yes…" he said.

He was giving me his best patronizing look, but I said to him that when I was dead, they'd be forced to add my name to their bloody list.

"And why is that?"

"Because I'll write a letter to a lawyer. I'll tell him to put it in my will. The last wishes of the deceased have to be respected."

"Not necessarily, Germain, not necessarily."

I don't care, I know what I'm talking about. I thought about it as I was walking home: when I die (when the Good Lord calls me, His hour will be my hour), I want my name to be engraved. Fifth on the list. Fifth from the top, while we're at it, no cheating. They can sort it out however they like, the bastards at the town hall. A will is a will and that's all there is to it. Yes, I said to myself, I'll do it, I'll write that letter. And I'll insist that it is engraved by Devallée personally just to wind him up. I'll go and see Maître Olivier and we'll talk about it. He's a lawyer, he should know what to do, shouldn't he?

B UT THE FACT REMAINS that on that particular Monday—the one when I first met Margueritte—I wasn't thinking about the war memorial, I had other things on my mind. I'd decided to buy some seeds and walk through the park on my way home to count the pigeons. It's more complicated than it sounds: even if you creep up quietly and stand completely still while you're counting, it's useless, they're always flapping about and getting agitated. They can be a real pain in the arse, pigeons.

If they carry on like that, I'll stick to counting the swans. For one thing, they don't move around as much, and for another, it's easier: there's only three.

So, anyway, Margueritte was sitting on this bench under the linden tree in front of the lawn. When I saw this little old lady who looked like she was the sort to throw breadcrumbs to get them to come to her, my heart sank. Another day wasted, I thought. I'd have to put off my bird-counting until tomorrow. Or until some day appointed by the Lord in His wisdom.

Counting pigeons requires stillness, so if someone comes along and gets them all flustered, you might as well just give up. They're very sensitive, these birds, they can tell when someone is looking at them. It's incredible how touchy they are. You might say conceited. The minute you look at them they start hopping around, they flutter about, they puff out their feathers...

But as it turned out, no. Which just goes to show how wrong you can be. About people, God, old ladies and pigeons.

The birds didn't do their usual song and dance for her. They stayed in a group, very well behaved. She didn't toss them crumbs bleating *here chickee-chickee-chickeeeee*!
She didn't stare at me out of the corner of her eye the way most people do when I count.

She stayed very still. But then, just as I was about to leave, she said:

"Nineteen."

Since I was only a few metres away, I heard her perfectly. I said:

"Are you talking to me?"

"I was saying there are nineteen. That little one, with the black feather in his tail, do you see him? Well, he's new. He's only been here since Saturday."

I was pretty impressed: she had the same total as I did. I said:

"So you like counting pigeons too?"

She cupped her hand to her ear and said:

"What did you say?"

I yelled:

"So-you-count-ing-pige-ons-too?"

"Of course I count them, young man. But there's no need to shout, I'll have you know. Just speak slowly and articulate... Well, a little louder than normal if it's not too much trouble."

It made me laugh, hearing someone call me "young man". That said, thinking about it, it wasn't as dumb as it sounded. People think I look young or old, depending. Depending on who's talking to me. It's normal: everything is relative—*something that is true only when considered in relation to something else*.

For someone as old as Margueritte, I was young, that was definite, as well as being relative.

When I sat down next to her, I realized she really was a tiny little old granny. People sometimes say things like "knee high to a grasshopper" without thinking. But in her case, it wasn't much of an exaggeration: her feet didn't even touch the ground. Whereas I'm forced to stretch my lanky legs out in front of me.

I asked her politely:

"Do you come here often?"

She smiled.

"Almost every day the Good Lord sends…"

"Are you a nun?"

She shook her head, startled.

"A nun? Good Lord no! Whatever made you think that?"

"I don't know. You mentioned the Good Lord, so… I just thought, maybe."

I felt a bit stupid. But it's not an insult to call someone a nun. Or at least not for someone old like her. Besides, she didn't seem annoyed.

I said:

"It's weird, I've never seen you here."

"As a rule, I tend to come a little earlier. But, if you don't mind my saying so, I have seen you here once or twice."

I said:

"Ah!"

I don't see what else I could have said apart from that.

She said:

"So, you like pigeons."

"Yes. Mostly I just like counting them."

"Oh, that… that's an onerous task. It requires repeated computations…"

She had a complicated way of talking, with more frills and laces than a tart's knickers, the way posh people talk. Then again, old people tend to be more smooth and polished than young people.

It's strange: as I said that I was thinking about river stones and how they're *smooth* and *polished*, precisely because they're *old*. Sometimes the same words can describe completely different things that turn out to be the same when you think about them for a while.

I know what I mean.

To show her I wasn't a moron, I said:

"I noticed him too, the little one with the black feather. So I named him Black Feather. The other birds don't really let him get at the food, have you noticed?"

"That's true. So you give them names?"

She seemed interested.

Believe it or not, this was when I first realized what it felt like for someone to be interested in you. If you've never felt it, I can tell you: it feels weird. Obviously, sometimes when I'm explaining something, people say: No, really? Are you serious? My God, that's terrible... But I'm talking about things that are really about me. Like for example the car that took a wrong turn at the hairpin bend on the coast road, one dead, three injured (I live right opposite, I'm usually the one who calls the ambulance, one time I even had to help the paramedics put a man who'd been cut to ribbons into a body bag, and it's a pretty crappy job let me tell you). Or I tell my friends that the men down at the factory have threatened to barricade the slip road off the motorway—I know this because Annette works at the warehouse—local news stories, you know the kind of thing. Current affairs. But the idea of someone being interested in *me*? Wow! I felt a lump in my throat like I was a little kid. I nearly burst into tears, that's how bad it was. If there's one thing that makes me uncomfortable, it's crying. Thankfully, it's not something that happens to me often, except this one day when I crushed my foot when Landremont and me were helping his sister move house and he dropped the chest of drawers and pretended like his hands were all sweaty. Anyone would have been in tears: it hurt like a bitch, even if it is only an anecdote. I'm talking real tears. Like when I came first in the regional finals in the orienteering race, just ahead of Cyril Gontier, a complete scumbag who made my life a misery all through primary school. Or the night I fell in love with Annette, which was pretty surprising because we'd been fucking for three months already. But that night, it was so beautiful, coming with her, that I had tears in my eyes.

Long story short, I don't know about you, but me, I'm ashamed to cry. My nose starts streaming snot worse than a two-year-old, my eyes piss tears like a fountain, I yowl like a bull in a slaughterhouse. Everything about me is in proportion to my huge size, which is good for the ladies, but it's also true when I'm upset, which is bad for me.

This little old lady made me all emotional without even trying. I don't know why, maybe it was the kindly way she said, So you give them names? Or maybe because she looked so gentle. And maybe it had something to do with the fact that I'd had a skinful at Jojo Zekouc's fortieth the night before and only had four hours' sleep. But like I said before, when you start with *maybes*, there's no end to it.

So, anyway, I said:

"Yes. I give them all names. It's easier to count them that way."

She raised her eyebrows.

"Well, well… Excuse me if I'm being indiscreet, but I have to confess I'm intrigued: how do you manage to tell them apart?"

"Um, well… It's a bit like with kids… Have you got children?"

"No. And you?"

"Me neither."

She nodded and smiled.

"In which case it is indeed an astute comparison…"

I wasn't really sure what this meant, but she seemed to want to know more, so I carried on:

"Actually, they're all different... If you don't really pay attention, you're not likely to notice, but if you study them carefully, you see that no two are the same. They've got their own personalities, even their own way of flying. That's why I said it's like kids. If you had kids, I'm sure you wouldn't get them mixed up..."

She gave a little laugh.

"Oh, if I had nineteen of them, I'm not so sure..."

This made me laugh too.

I don't often laugh when I'm with women. Not old women, at any rate.

It's strange, I felt like we were friends, the two of us. Well, not really, but something quite like it. Since then, I've tracked down the word I needed: *allies*.

Words are boxes that we use to store thoughts the better to present them to others. Show them to their best advantage. For example, on days when you just feel like kicking anything that moves, you can just sulk. Problem is, people might think you're ill, or depressed. Whereas if you just say out loud: Don't piss me around, I'm really not in the mood today! It avoids all sorts of confusion.

Or, to take a different example, some girl sets your head spinning, you think about her every minute of every day the Good Lord sends, at times like this it feels like your brain has taken up residence in your dick, but if you just tell her I love you like crazy etc., etc., it can help a little when it comes to dealing with it.

And yet what should matter is not the wrapping but what you put inside.

There are beautiful gift-wrapped packages with pathetic shit inside, and crudely wrapped packages that contain real treasures. That's why, when it comes to words, I'm suspicious, you understand?

Thinking back, it was probably best that I didn't know too many words. I didn't need to choose: I simply said what I knew how to say. That way, I didn't run the risk of making a mistake. And more important, I didn't have to think so hard.

All the same—and this is something I only realized since

Margueritte, I think—having the right words can be useful when you want to express yourself.

Ally, that was the word I was looking for that day. At the same time, if I'd known it, it wouldn't really have changed anything. About how I felt, I mean.

T HAT MONDAY, I told Margueritte the names of all my birds. Well, the ones that were there, because actually there are twenty-six that hang out in the park. I'm only talking regular visitors here. Not the migrant birds that flutter in, crash-land on the lawn and pounce on the breadcrumbs like they've got no manners and get a good thrashing from the regulars. I started:

"That one there is Pierrot. Next to him is Headstrong… Bullseye, Thievish, Sweetie… That one there is Verdun. The little brown one is Capuchin… That's Cachou… Princess… Margueritte…"

"Just like me!" she said.

"Sorry?"

"My name is Margueritte too."

It was weird to think that here I was talking to a Margueritte while another Margueritte, feathered from beak to backside, was pecking at an apple core at my feet.

I thought, Now *there's* a coincidence!

It's a word I only learned the meaning of recently: every time Landremont comes into Chez Francine and sees me at the bar having a drink with Jojo Zekouc, he taps me on the shoulder and says:

"Well, well. Germain sitting at a bar? Now, *there's* a coincidence!"

I used to think it was his way of saying, Hi, nice to

see you. But, no, apparently, it meant he thought I was a pathetic drunk clinging to the bar like a limpet to a rock. Jojo explained the real meaning to me one day. He said:

"Our friend Landremont seems to think we're a couple of alcoholics."

I asked why he said that. He explained.

Landremont is not a friend. One week he's playing belote with you and treating you like a brother, then Saturday night he'll end up punching you in the face. When he drinks too much, he gets addled.

Whenever he refers to Landremont, Marco calls him the weather vane. Jojo says he's as changeable as the wind. Francine thinks he's a crackpot. I used to think that meant as cracked as the pot, which sounded about right. But I also agree with the other definition: *someone who suffers changeable, often disturbing mood swings; see also: capricious, whimsical, fickle.*

That said, it's probably down to him that I learned most things before I met Margueritte. He's read a hell of a lot, has Landremont. His place is crammed with books. Not just in the toilet, and not just magazines.

He could teach Jacques Devallée a thing or two. Maybe even the mayor, who knows?

L ANDREMONT IS A LITTLE, nervous guy with scrawny arms. He's bald on top but has hairy arms. Thick bushy hair that's not really blond but not quite white.

His poor wife passed away from ovarian cancer, which is a complete bitch… Ever since, he's been nursing his grief by damaging his liver, though he does it hypocritically, on the sly. When he's with us, he'll just have half a lager, a small white wine, a shot of Mauresque, a couple of glasses of pastis, just for the sake of appearances.

He even makes snide comments like, Well, well! What a coincidence!

It doesn't matter, everyone knows where they stand with him since the night Marco's car broke down.

This one night, Marco was supposed to be going round to dinner with his sister and his brother-in-law. Just when he was about to set off, his Mercedes conked out. Marco went round to Landremont's place and was hammering on the door for ten minutes before he answered. Marco kept knocking because he could see lights on and hear the TV. Given that they're neighbours, he knew Landremont was definitely at home.

Anyway, long story short, in the end Landremont came to the door.

Marco told us about it the day after.

"Straight up, lads, I thought I'd met a zombie! Landremont had had a skinful!… I told him I really needed a favour, that I needed to be somewhere and I couldn't get the car started. Said maybe it was a track rod or maybe the cylinder head, or maybe it was something else. And d'you know what he said to me?"

We said: No.

It was true, we didn't know.

"He said: 'Leave me the hell alone, go find a mechanic.'"

Marco added, "I've never seen a guy in such a state, never! And I've been on my fair share of benders, anyone here can vouch for that."

We said: Oh, yeah, no question…

"Hang on, I'm not finished! He's so bombed that at one point he says: 'Sorry Marco, I need to take a piss.' So I said: 'Sure, no problem, go ahead.' But he just stands there, not moving, holding the door open. You want to know the best part?"

We said: What?

"He pissed himself. He stood there, stiff as a board, looking like he was thinking, and the bastard pissed in his pants!"

We all said: Really?!

Michel said:

"So what did you do?"

"What could I do? I said goodnight and I went home. Then I called my brother-in-law and asked him to come pick me up."

We asked: What about the car?

"Pff, some glitch with the electrics, that's all."

Ever since then, we've known that Landremont has rough nights.

WHILE I WAS EXPLAINING the names of the birds to Margueritte, I wasn't thinking about any of that, just about the word *coincidence*, which reminded me of Landremont's comment when he saw me having a drink with Jojo. Which brought me back to Jojo, specifically to his birthday party the previous night (well, five in the morning, actually). And the fact I hadn't had much sleep, which, on the one hand, explained why I was so emotional, and on the other, why I had a banging headache. If I don't get my eight hours, I'm a train wreck the whole day.

It was at this point the little old lady said:

"You're looking very thoughtful…"

So I went and explained everything, like we were close friends or something.

"No, not really… Just a bit tired. Last night, I was at the fortieth birthday of my friend Jojo Zekouc."

And so she said:

"So you've got a friend who's a cook?"

I was gobsmacked.

"So you know Jojo?" I said.

"No, I haven't had the pleasure. Why do you ask?"

"Well, how did you know he's a cook if you've never met him?"

"Well, because of his name, I suppose. Zekouc sounds like *the cook* in English."

"Oh, yeah," I said, "of course."

But I was completely stunned. I mean, obviously I knew that that kind of thing was possible.

When I was a kid, the butcher on the place Jules-Ferry was called Duporc. And the guy in the hardware shop opposite the town hall is called Le Charpentier. But it would never have occurred to me that Jojo had a name that matched his job. And an English name to boot.

I said goodbye to Margueritte. Since she was a nice person, I added:

"Margueritte is a pretty name."

"For a pigeon, certainly!" she said and laughed.

I giggled. She said:

"What about you, what is your name?… If I may be so forward."

"Germain Chazes."

And then, as if I was the mayor or something, she said:

"Well then, Monsieur Chazes, it has been a pleasure to make your acquaintance."

She gestured to the birds and said: "And thank you for introducing me to your little brood."

I thought to myself, she's funny.

We left it at that.

As soon as I left the park, I went straight to Chez Francine, because this thing about the English cook was bothering me. On Mondays, Jojo's shift starts a little earlier. They treat me like family there. Whenever I want to see him, I just go round the counter and into the back.

I ran smack bang into him. He was peeling vegetables. So I laughed and I said to him:

"Hey! You really picked the right job, what with your name and all."

He seemed surprised and asked what I meant. I didn't want to make a big deal of it, I wasn't trying to make fun of him, so I just said wasn't it funny that he ended up working in a restaurant given his surname.

"With my surname? Pelletier? Sorry, I don't get it…"

"What's with the 'Pelletier'? Who said anything about Pelletier, I meant your surname, Zekouc. Did you know that Zekouc was English?"

"Oh, OK, I get it… It's a joke! Good one, Germain," he said, laughing.

I had the feeling I was missing something.

I was a bit upset that I couldn't work it out. But it was hardly the first time: I often feel that some of the things people are saying go right over my head (that's obviously a figure of speech, given how tall I am). Sometimes, I understand everything that's been said. Sometimes just part of it. Most of the time, not much.

When I was a kid, my mother used to call me the happy halfwit. But it wasn't true; I wasn't happy. Halfwit, maybe. But *happy*, no way.

Landremont tells me I'm smart enough to know how stupid I am, and that's the root of my misfortune. I think he's probably right, even if, thinking about it, it's not exactly a compliment. Anyway, I can tell when there's something I don't understand.

Annette says she's just the same, but it's only with maths and sums in her case.

My mother also used to call me the retard or the idiot. And when I started to grow up: you stupid bastard.

She didn't have an ounce of maternal fibre, as my friend Julien says.

Julien was my best mate from back in primary school. He'd often come home with me. We'd spend the afternoons playing at my house. This was before I walked out, before I left her to her scrapbooks and cleared off to live my own life.

When Julien came round, he could see for himself that my mother wasn't the maternal type… Not that I ever wanted for anything as regards food or hygiene. But there's ways and ways of serving soup, and after a while the soup plate looks like a dog's bowl. And the clips round the ear never did "sort out my ideas". Not for me, not for anyone. You've either got ideas or you haven't. Beatings hurt, that's all they do.

And the thing that hurts the most is having to hold back, never hitting back, even when you're taller than her and you could shut her up with a little tap, or slam her against the wall.

But if there's one thing I can't accuse my mother of, it's being two-faced. Absolutely not. She always told me exactly what she thought of me. Not that that made it any easier.

I STILL HADN'T worked out what it was I was missing when Landremont came into the restaurant. I whistled for him to come and join us. I said to him:

"Don't you think that, with a name like his, Jojo here was right to become a chef?"

Landremont looked at me like he was puzzled. Then suddenly he said:

"Oh, you mean because of Pelletier Crispbread'."

Pelletier must have been his mother's name and Zekouc his father's. It does sound slightly Arabic—even if it is supposedly English—so maybe he doesn't want everyone to know. Not that Francine has a racist bone in her body. Youssef should know.

I said to Landremont:

"No, I meant his other name. Now you mention it, Pelletier is pretty funny too. But 'Zekouc' means *the cook* in English, in case you didn't already know."

I was proud of myself.

Landremont burst out laughing. He clapped me on the back and said:

"Jesus, you're dumb as pigshit! You're dumb as a sack of hammers. There's nothing going on in that head of yours—"

"Cut it out!" said Jojo.

Landremont was laughing so hard he had tears in his eyes.

Jojo coughed to clear his throat. I could tell he was embarrassed. He put on that voice people use with five-year-olds when they want to explain something. When people talk to me like that, it pisses me off like you can't imagine.

"Germain, my surname is Pel-le-tier. Joël Pelletier. People call me Zekouc because I'm the cook… But it's only a nickname, you knew that?"

"Of course!" I said, "Of course I knew that, what do you take me for?"

He gave me a wink.

"I know you knew. I'm only explaining for Landremont's benefit."

"Yeah, right," said Landremont.

Then we changed the subject.

I felt hacked off, though I didn't show it.

It's exhausting always having to watch life without a decoder, as Marco puts it sometimes.

If being intelligent was just about making the effort, I'd be a genius, take it from me. Because I've made a lot of effort. A lot of effort. But it's like trying to dig a trench with a soup spoon. Everyone else has a JCB digger, and I'm standing there like an idiot. It's the only word for it.

THAT NIGHT, I didn't hang out with them. When Julien showed up about ten o'clock and said, So what about it, shall we carry on where we left off last night? I said no, I had some shopping to do.

"At ten o'clock at night? Or maybe you're not buying, maybe you're making… a delivery?" said Landremont, grabbing his balls through his trousers. "If it's the shop I'm thinking of, don't worry, it stays open all night. Oh, and give Annette my love, will you?"

"Fuck off." I said.

He laughed. He was acting the smartarse, said I was right, women are like bottles of booze: to be sampled, savoured, and slung out!

He can be pretty crude sometimes.

I said:

"You'd know all about… bottles of booze."

Jojo whistled from the kitchen:

"Ho ho! You scored a direct hit there, Germain! And a good one, too!"

"You just got bitch-slapped," said Marco, turning to Landremont.

Landremont just shrugged, but he was angry and that made me happy.

Francine, in the middle of wiping down the bar, chuckled and said:

"What do you expect? Germain is the smartest of the lot of you. And the kindest, too! You don't pay them any heed, they're just jealous. Isn't that right, Germain?"

I said yes and went over and kissed her on the cheek. Francine always stands up for me, I think she's fond of me. I think it might be more than that, but just in case I'm mistaken, I've no intention of finding out. Besides, Youssef is a nice guy, I'm not about to do the dirty on him behind his back, it's just common decency.

And anyway, she's a bit old for my taste.

I went over to Annette's place, obviously. And not just to do it. Annette relaxes me. Though in a manner of speaking: when we meet up, it's not to play Ludo.

I remember the first time for her and me was after a May Day festival. The two of us had danced together, then a thunderstorm broke. It started bucketing down. The wind started howling, the temperature dropped suddenly. Annette had parked her car next to the square, she suggested she could drive us all back. We said yes. Given the weather, we weren't going to pass up a lift. Besides, it was sensible, given the state of Marco, who was drunk as a skunk.

We dropped off Marco and Landremont first, just outside the village. Then we made a U-turn to drop off Julien and his girlfriend Létitia, who's not his girlfriend any more, but he didn't lose on the deal dumping her for Céline. Because his old girlfriend was a complete bitch. We're allowed to say it now, there's a statue of limitations.

So, we ended up outside my place. And Annette said:

"Doesn't that caravan of yours leak in weather like this?"

"No, never. But I'll be freezing my arse off tonight, I can tell you. The radiator is banjaxed and I didn't get round to buying a new one. Why would I? It's the beginning of May…"

"Do you want to spend the night at my place?" she said.

And seeing as how she put her hand on my thigh as she said it, and I was horny as hell from all the slow dances, I said yes. What would you have done in my position?

I'd never been to Annette's place before. I thought it was nicely decorated, but I wasn't here to take the grand tour. Annette made us some coffee, then she came and sat next to me. I was wondering how I was going to lead up to things, but she made the first move. I wasn't even shocked. Still, it's something I don't really like—girls whose way of saying hello is to throw themselves at you. It's not very feminine in my opinion. Then again, I have to admit it's very practical. Well, that's the way I used to see things. I was pretty rough around the edges back then. There's been a lot of polishing since. I don't see things like I used to, and that goes for sex too. My brain is up here and my balls are down there and I don't get the two mixed up any more.

Annette is small and she looks really skinny. She's thirty-six, but she really doesn't look it. It's stupid, but I was afraid of hurting her. I'm a big lunk, and I was worried about whether I'd suffocate her if I got on top, whether she was big enough to take me inside her, whether I'd tear her or I don't know what. It was all in my head, but it worried me all the same. Overthinking ruins your performance.

There are times when it's best to be spontaneous.

She's really weirdly built, Annette: she's got a tiny waist I could circle with my hands, and breasts pumped up with helium that are round and firm and fill your whole palm and can't be squashed, you can take my word for it. And she's got long legs for her height, a little arse as firm and round as a cabbage. She's not pretty exactly, what with the dark rings round her eyes, her thin face and that hangdog look, but there's something about her. Landremont says she's got an arse that could make a fortune and a face that could lose one. He's in no position to talk, given that his own wife was a horse-faced bitch. God rest her soul, may the Good Lord gather her to Himself, she was a hell of a decent woman.

So, anyway, that night, Annette made the first move and I didn't smother her or crush her or do anything else unforeseen. When I found myself inside her, it was all cotton, silk and feathers. So warm and soft, so perfectly snug I could have spent my whole life there. A bit later, we did it again. She devoured me with her eyes. She was gentle with me, she did everything she could to please me. She told me she had been dreaming of me for a long time. It's weird, when a girl says that, especially if she says it with tears in her eyes and a quaver in her voice as her hand is gently taking care of you.

It was almost embarrassing. But nice.

WHEN I FIRST knew Annette, I'd never really taken much of an interest in women. I either thought of girls as friends and I didn't touch, or I thought of them as Kleenex and I didn't care. I'm not proud, but I'm not ashamed, that's just the way I was. The Germain I was back then is gone, and good riddance.

I've changed. Since I met Margueritte, I've been exercising my intelligence. I ask myself questions about life, and then I try to answer them, concentrating without cheating. I think about existence. About what I had when I started out, and everything I've had to work out for myself since.

Of the words I've learned, there are two I particularly remember: *innate, acquired*.

Without looking them up in the dictionary again, I'd be hard pushed to give you a precise definition, but I remember the gist. "Innate" is what people have when they're born, and it's easy to remember because it's *in* your *nature*. "Acquired" is what we spend the rest of our lives struggling to learn. The stuff we're supposed to pick up from other people along the way. But from who?

For example, emotions are not innate, not at all. Eating and drinking, yeah, sure, that's instinct. If you don't do it, you die. But emotions are an optional extra, or you can do without. I should know. It's a poor excuse for a life, you're half-witted, not much different from a dumb animal, but you can go on living a long time just the same. A very long time. I don't want to be always using myself as an example, but when I was starting out in life, I didn't get much in the way of affection.

In a normal family—from what I've seen—people cry sometimes, and they scream, but there are moments of tenderness, people ruffle your hair, they say things like, Would you look at the state of him, he's the spitting image of his father! And they pretend like they're angry but they're just teasing because really they're proud they know where you come from. I've seen it when Marco talks about his daughter or Julien talks about his two sons.

Me, I don't come from anywhere, that's my problem. Obviously I had to come from some guy's balls, it's not like there's an alternative. And from some woman's pussy, like everyone else on this earth. But in my case, as soon as I was born, the good part was over. Done and dusted. That's why I say that emotions are *acquired*, they're something you have to learn. If it took me longer than it took most people, it's because I didn't have a role model in the beginning. I had to find everything out for myself. And it's the same with speech, I learned to speak on building sites and in bars mostly, which is why I have trouble explaining things—I use too many swear words, and I don't always explain things the right way round like educated people: first *a*, then *b*, then *c*.

When Landremont, or Devallée, or the mayor (who's also a secondary school teacher) talk about something, you can tell they've got a firm grasp on the idea. After that, all they need to do is reel it in, keep following it until they get to the other end. It's called not losing the thread. You can interrupt them, you can butt in with *From what I've heard…* or *By all accounts…*, it makes no bloody difference, they still steer a steady course!

Me, I always stray from the point. I start off with one thing, that leads to another and another and another, and by the time I get to the end of the sentence, I don't even remember what I was talking about. And if I get interrupted, I get even more confused and end up in a complete muddle.

When educated people lose their way while they're explaining something, they go pale. They put a finger to their lips and they frown and they say, Damn it, where was I? What was I saying again?

And everyone around them looks worried, they hold their breath as though this was something serious…

The difference between them and me is that, when I lose the thread, no one gives a toss.

Including me. In fact, especially me.

B EFORE, I used to be functionally illiterate—*Being unable to read or write; see also: ignorant*—but I'm not ashamed. Reading is something that's acquired. You don't even need to go looking: when you're little, you're sent to school where they force-feed you, like they do with geese.

Some teachers are good at it, they've got the skill, the patience, that kind of thing. They gradually fill up your memory until it's chock-a-block. With others, it's gobble or die! They stuff you full of information without bothering to worry where it's going to end up. And what happens? A crumb of information goes down the wrong way, and you choke on it. All you want is to spit it out and starve rather than feel this way again.

My teacher, Monsieur Bayle, was a vicious force-feeder. He scared the crap out of me. There were days when he only had to look at me and I'd nearly piss myself. Just the way he said my name: *Chazes!* I knew he didn't like me. He must have had his reasons. For a teacher, having a halfwit pupil must be a pain in the arse. I can understand that. So, he took out his frustration by making me come up to the blackboard every day. I had to recite my lessons.

I had to recite my lessons in front of the arse-lickers, who elbowed each other and jeered with their hands in front of their mouths, but also in front of the dunces, who were relieved to see that I was dumber than them. Monsieur

Bayle never helped, in fact he did the opposite, he made things worse. He was a real bastard. I can still hear him now, I don't even have to try, his voice is permanently drilling into my ear.

"What's the matter, Chazes? Your brain still in bed?"

"What's up Chazes, too cool for school?"

"It seems that young Chazes is up excrement creek!"

This would make my classmates laugh.

Then, he would add:

"Well, Chazes? I'm waiting, we're all waiting, your friends are waiting…"

He would shift his chair just a little to turn it towards me. He would fold his arms and stare at me, nodding his head. He would tap the floor with the toe of his shoe, saying nothing. Tap, tap, tap… was the only sound I heard, that and the tick-tock, tick-tock of the clock on the wall. Sometimes it went on for so long that the other boys finally shut up.

The silence engulfing the tick-tock and the tapping of the shoe was so great that I would hear my heart pounding in my head. Eventually, he would sigh and wave me back to my seat, saying:

"Decidedly, my dear Chazes, I fear you're a few cards short of a deck."

The other boys roared with laughter, enjoying the spectacle. Me, I wanted to kill myself. Or to kill him, if I could have. Killing him would have been better. Grinding the bastard's head under my large boot like the chalk-dusted cockroach he was. At night, in bed, I would revel in these murderous thoughts, it was the only time I felt happy. If I didn't grow up to be violent—or no more violent than necessary, anyway—it's no thanks to him. Sometimes, I think that thugs learn to be brutal because people have been cruel to them. If you want to make a dog vicious, all you have to do is beat him for no reason. It's the same with a kid, only easier. You don't even need to beat him. Jeering and mocking him is enough.

In primary school, there are kids who learn their conjugations and their multiplication tables. Me, I learned something more useful: the strong get off on walking all over other people, and wiping their feet while they're at it, like you would on a doormat. This is what I learned from my years at school. It was a hell of a lesson. All that because of some bastard who didn't like kids. Or at least he didn't like me. Maybe my life would have been different if I'd had a different teacher. Who knows? I'm not saying it's his fault I'm a moron, I'm pretty sure I was one even before that. But he made my life a misery. I can't help thinking that other teachers would have given me a hand up. Something I could use to grab on to, instead of sliding down to the bottom of the hole. But unfortunately there were only two classes in the school back then, one for the babies and one for the bigger kids. We were stuck with Bayle from age eight to age ten. (Eleven, in my case.) I know I wasn't the only one who got it in the neck. There were other kids whose lives he ruined with his meanness and his cruelty. He was full of himself just because he was a teacher. He looked down on us, which

45

wasn't exactly hard since we were only kids and didn't know anything. But instead of being proud, of being happy about all the things he could teach us, he humiliated the weak, the dunces, all those who really needed him.

To be that much of a bastard takes talent, I think.

Y OU CAN SAY what you like, but, for a kid, schooldays aren't the happiest days of your life. Anyone who says different doesn't like kids, or doesn't remember what it was like to be one.

What makes kids happy is fishing for gudgeon or building gravel barriers on the tracks to derail goods trains—even if everyone knows it never works. Or climbing up the strut of a bridge from the bank (which doesn't work either, because of the slant). Jumping off the top of the cemetery wall, setting fire to a patch of waste ground, knocking on doors and running away. Making little kids eat 'sweets' that are really goat droppings. That kind of thing.

When you're a kid, all you want is to be a hero.

If your parents aren't standing behind you, banging on about how school is important, how you have to go, how you've got no choice, well, you don't bother—at least I didn't—or you go as little as possible.

My mother wasn't strict about stuff like that. She would have broken a brush handle over my head if I'd tracked mud into the hall, but I don't think she gave a damn that I never learned to read and write. When I came home at five o'clock, she hardly even looked at me. Her first words were always:

"Did you get the bread?"

And the next words were:

"Don't leave your stuff lying around. Go and put your schoolbag away."

I didn't need to be told twice. I tossed my bag at the foot of my bed and went out to play with my mates, or by myself.

The older I got, the more I bunked off. When Bayle asked me where I'd been, I'd give him some lame excuse: my mother was sick and I had to do the shopping, my grandmother had just died, I'd sprained my ankle, I'd been bitten by a rabid dog, I'd had to go to the doctor.

I trained myself to lie and look him straight in the face. It's harder than you think, when you're only ten and you're not very broad in the shoulders yet. But it taught me about courage. That's something it's important to have in life.

It didn't matter, Bayle was happy to let me fool him. It was better than having me causing trouble in his class, and it gave him a bit of a rest from constantly yelling *Chazes, can you repeat what I just said?* knowing full well I couldn't. What all this meant was by the end of primary school, I was more likely to be off fishing somewhere than warming my arse on a school bench. This meant that later, when I joined the army, I was classed as suffering from mental retardation, a phrase that neatly contains the word they really thought described me: *retard*.

In the period I was talking about just now, the period when I first got together with Annette, life pretty much went right over my head. And it didn't bother me. I didn't ask questions. I did my business in the sack and elsewhere, I played cards, I got hammered every Saturday night and dried out during the week, I took jobs on building sites when I was strapped for cash, life seemed straightforward. I made no real connection between living life and understanding life, if you see what I mean.

It's like with cars: if someone asked you to change the distributor, the coupling, the drive belt—or even just top up the oil, it doesn't matter—how would you fare? Because most people who can drive don't know the first thing about how or why an engine works. That was pretty much how I looked at my life. I turned the steering wheel, changed the gears, filled up when I needed to, and that was all…

When I met Margueritte, at first I found learning stuff complicated. Then intriguing. Then depressing, because learning to think is like getting glasses when you're blind as a bat. Everything around was comforting, it was simple, blurry. Now suddenly you see all the cracks, the rust, the rot, you can see that everything is crumbling. You see death, you realize that you're going to have to leave all this behind, and probably in a way that won't be fun. You realize that time doesn't just pass, every day pushes you one step closer to kicking the bucket. There's no high score that gives you a free game. You do your circuit, and that's it, you're history.

Honestly, for some people, life is a complete con job.

MARGUERITTE SAYS that cultivating your mind is like climbing a mountain. I understand that better now. When you're down in the valley, you think you see everything and know everything about the world: the meadows, the grass, the cow dung (that last example is mine). One fine day, you pick up your backpack and start walking. What you leave behind gets smaller the farther you travel: the cows shrink to the size of rabbits, to ants, to flyspecks. Meanwhile the landscape you discover as you climb seems bigger and bigger. You thought the world ended with the mountain, but it doesn't! Behind it, there is another mountain, and another a little higher, and still another. And then a whole range. The valley where you were living a peaceful life was just one valley among many, and not even the biggest. Actually, it was the arsehole of the universe. As you walk, you meet other people, but the closer you come to the summit, the fewer are still climbing alongside you and the more you freeze your balls off! That's just another figure of speech. Once you're at the top, you're happy, you think you're clever because you've climbed higher than everyone else. You can see for miles. The only thing is, after a while, you realize something really stupid: you're all alone. All alone and insignificant.

From the Good Lord's point of view, even we are probably no bigger than bloody flyspecks.

This is probably what Margueritte means when she says, Do you know, Germain, culture can be very isolating?

I think she's right, and what's worse, you must feel very dizzy constantly looking down at the world below.

My plan is to stop halfway up the slope, and I'll be happy if I manage to climb that high. Margueritte has got education. And I'm not talking about the piss-poor education and a piece of paper that everyone's got (well, everyone except me), but the sort of higher-level education that takes so many years that you're old by the time you graduate and don't have time to make enough pension contributions to be able to retire.

Margueritte passed her doctorate, only she wasn't a *real* doctor, she worked with plants. She researched grape seeds. Personally, I can't really see what there is to research, I mean a seed is a seed, there's not much to it. But that's what she studied, so I shouldn't look down my nose at it.

There are no stupid professions, only bad seeds.

Anyway, maybe that's why she's always talking about *cultivating* and *cultivation*. Another pair of words that sound the same but mean different things.

In cultivation, you till the ground, you mark out your furrows, you aerate the soil where you sow your seeds. And then there's the cultivating Margueritte talks about where you just pick up a book and read. But that's not easy either, quite the opposite.

I can talk about books now: I've read some.

When you're functionally illiterate like me, you wouldn't believe how difficult it is to read. You look at the first word,

OK, you understand it, then the next, and with a bit of luck the next. You keep going, running your finger under the words, eight, nine, ten, twelve, until you get to a full stop. But when you get there, you're not better off! Because no matter how much you try to put everything together, you can't, the words are still jumbled up like a handful of nuts and bolts tossed into a box. For people who know what they're doing, it's easy. They just screw the right bits together. They're not fazed by fifteen words, twenty words, that's what they call a sentence. For me, for a long time, it was very different. I knew how to read, obviously, since I learned the alphabet. My problem was the meaning. A book was like a rat trap for my pride, a treacherous, two-faced thing that seemed harmless at first glance.

Nothing but ink and paper: big deal. Actually it was a wall. A brick wall to bang your head on.

So, obviously, I couldn't see the point of reading unless I had to, like for tax returns and social security forms.

I think this is what I found most intriguing—*see also: arousing one's curiosity*—about Margueritte.

Every time I saw her, either she was doing nothing or she had her nose in a book. And when she was doing nothing, it was only because she'd just put her book back in her handbag to chat to me.

That's something I realized after a while. These days, if you asked me what was in her little back handbag, I could reel off everything with my eyes closed and not make a single mistake: a packet of tissues, a pen, a box of mints, a book, her wallet, her purse, and some perfume in a small blue glass bottle.

Every single thing is always the same, except for the book, that changes.

When I look at Margueritte, it's funny, I don't see a little old lady who weighs about forty kilos, all crumpled like a poppy, her spine a little bent and her hands all shrivelled; I see that in her head she has thousands of bookshelves all carefully catalogued and numbered. And you wouldn't think to look at her that she's intelligent. I mean how intelligent she actually is. She talks to me about normal things, she walks in the park just like an ordinary person.

She's not at all stuck up.

But from what she tells me, when she was young, it was rare for a woman to do advanced studies. I still don't really know what she did exactly when she was researching seeds, or what the point of it was, but I know she worked in laboratories with microscopes and bottles and test tubes, and just thinking about it amazes me.

That and the books she is forever reading.

Well, that she was forever reading.

WE RAN INTO EACH OTHER again, Margueritte and me, I don't remember the exact date, it wasn't long after that first time. She was sitting on the same bench and it was probably the same time of day.

Seeing her in the distance, I thought, Hey, it's the pigeon lady, but I didn't think any more about it. I went over to say hello. Her eyes were half closed, she looked like she was thinking, or she could just as easily have been dozing.

With old people, everything ends up looking much the same: thinking, dying, napping...

I said hello. She turned, she smiled.

"Well, well. Hello, Monsieur Chazes."

Not many people round here call me *monsieur*.

It's more, Hi Germain! Or even, Hey Chazes!

She nodded for me to sit next to her. And that's when I saw she had a book in her lap. Seeing I was looking at it, trying to work out what it was from the picture on the cover, she asked:

"Do you like reading?"

"God, no."

It just came out, like a bullet from a gun, there was no way to take it back.

"No?"

She looked astonished, did Margueritte.

I tried to smooth things over, I said:

"Too much work."

"Ah, I see. It's true that, in life, work takes up a great deal of time… Counting pigeons, writing one's name on the war memorial…"

She said this like it was a private joke, she wasn't being nasty.

"You saw me doing that? I mean you saw me at the memorial?"

She nodded.

"That is to say… I did catch sight of you at the monument one day. You seemed utterly engrossed, but from here I could not guess what you were doing. So—and I hope you will forgive my curiosity—after you left, I went over to see for myself. And that is when I noticed that you had added a name to the list of the departed: Germain Chazes… Your father, I assume? Because, unless I've misremembered, you told me that your first name is Germain, didn't you?"

I said yes. But given it was a single yes and there was more than one question, she took it to mean what she wanted. And I suddenly found myself with a dead soldier with the same surname as me for a father, which should have felt weird. Chazes is my mother's surname, she was single when she got knocked up and she stayed single when she had me on her hands.

Or "got lumbered with me" as she often put it. Because I was a burden to my mother. And she made no bones about letting everyone know. But, as Landremont would say, the converse is reciprocal—or something like that—which means that she was a pain in the arse for me too.

I didn't want to disappoint Margueritte, to explain about the 14th July celebrations and my mother in the bushes learning about the birds and the bees from some thirty-year-old guy from the next village which left her with a bad reputation and a halfwit son. I got the impression that this wasn't the kind of thing that happened in Margueritte's world. That's why I said yes. And suddenly, I was a poor unfortunate orphan whose dad had died in the war, which sounds a lot classier than the result of some random shag, if you want my opinion.

She gave a little sigh, like she felt sorry for me.

Sorry about what? I wondered. What was there to feel sorry about? My life's pretty good, actually.

I remember she looked at me, all serious, and she said:

"I find it profoundly touching that you should be so passionate about righting what must seem a terrible injustice… In fact, when I think about it, it's absurd: if your father died during the Algerian War, why is his name not engraved on the memorial?"

What could I say, what sort of convincing excuse could I come up with to explain why my old man's name wasn't on the list? Given that, from what I know, his real name is Despuis, he was a carpenter and he didn't die in combat, he died in a car accident in Spain when I was about four or five. To say nothing of the fact that he'd never set foot in the Algerian War (1954–1962). And that if he'd died in the

Algerian War, I'd never have been born—which would have been a relief for all concerned—seeing as how I came into this world in April 1963. The 17th, to be exact.

But however much I thought about it, I couldn't find a way of piecing the truth together and presenting it for this little old lady. I sat there like a lemon, fretting over my version of the story, but I couldn't find a way to tart it up.

It was at this point she said:

"I'm so sorry, Monsieur Chazes… I realize my question was deeply indiscreet, please forgive me. I did not intend to make you feel uncomfortable. I'm sorry…"

I said:

"No harm done."

And it was true. I don't give a toss about my father. For me, he's just biology.

T HAT DAY, as I headed home, I wondered why I was so obsessed with adding my name on that stupid slab of marble. Because deep down, if I really thought about it—something I didn't much like doing back then—I knew perfectly well I'd never committed war. And I knew that you had to be dead to be on the list. Even if I played the idiot for Devallée, the deputy mayor.

I, Germain Chazes, knew that only people who'd snuffed it had a right to be there, engraved in capital letters, being shat on by the pigeons from the park.

Why then was I so obsessed with being one of them? Maybe so I'd feel that I belonged, that I existed even just a little bit, even if I wasn't really indelible on all surfaces. Or maybe so someone would say, Hey, who is this guy who's always writing his name on the war memorial? I wonder why he does it?

I would have liked to talk about all this stuff to someone, but who? Landremont or Marco would be a waste of time, they'd have thought I was stupid, just for a change. Julien, I wasn't sure about. Or Jojo, or Youssef. Maybe Annette?

Yeah, maybe it was the sort of thing you could talk about with a woman.

Women are funny: they don't have a clue about anything, you just have to look at the way they let us take advantage of them, but for some things, they've got, like, a sixth sense.

In two seconds flat, they can tell you exactly what makes you tick. And it's not always wrong, the stuff they come out with. They talk a lot of sense sometimes.

All of a sudden, I noticed something incredible: here I was thinking about the way I think, the way I react, that kind of stuff. Bloody hell! I thought.

This was new to me, it made me dizzy. Because, before that day, I was either thinking or not thinking. One or the other. And when I was thinking, I didn't think about it, it was like it happened outside me. When I thought, I did it without thinking.

OK, I realize that when you put it that way it doesn't make much sense. But I wasn't in the habit of trying to work out the how and the why of things.

By accident, Margueritte had triggered a burning desire for thinking, it was like my brain had a hard on.

So, that night, while I was barbecuing my steak outside the caravan, I remembered a whole bunch of things that happened since I was a kid. That stuff I told you about Monsieur Bayle for example. The screaming matches with my mother. That bastard Gardini—I'll tell you about him later. The first time I snatched a handbag, but I was just a kid, all boys do stuff like that. The army. Boozy games of belote and bar fights. Getting legless and getting a leg over. All the arseholes who make fun of me and think I don't notice.

And the years that went by so fast that now, as Landremont says, what with statistics and life expectancy, I'm closer to the end than to the start.

Later, I remembered all the things I wanted to be when I was a kid. Even the vocation—*Inclination, penchant (for a particular profession or occupation)*—I had when I was about twelve. Whenever it was open, I found an excuse to pop into the church. Not to pray—I didn't give a damn whether the Good Lord in His mercy forgave me. I went in to look at the big rose window above the altar. I thought the colours were mind-blowing and the images were amazing. So I decided to be a rose window-maker.

When I said this during careers guidance, I was told that "rose window-maker" was not a profession. Not a profession? What the hell was wrong with these people? It's the most wonderful profession in the world. Instead, they suggested I could apprentice with a glassmaker. I told them to go screw themselves, I said I wasn't interested in making glasses. Why not somewhere that made Pyrex bowls while they were at it?

It was one word, just one word, to work out. But that day, no one bothered to explain that you had to be a glassmaker to make rose windows.

So, anyway, as I was chopping tomatoes and onions for a salad, I thought some more about me, but as though it wasn't me. As though it was some guy I'd bumped into on the street, the neighbours' kid, a nephew. A lad who hadn't had much luck in life. A poor bastard who had no father and no mother to speak of, because if I had to choose between my mother or no mother...

I saw myself from above and it felt peculiar. I thought, Jesus H. Christ, Germain, why do you do the things you do?

By "things" I meant: counting pigeons, running until I was out of breath, playing belote, whittling bits of wood with my Opinel. I asked myself the question seriously, it was like I was someone else talking. The voice of God, maybe—with all due respect and reverence to Him. *Germain, why do you do the things you do?* It echoed inside my head. *Why, Germain, why?*

I think I had a sort of brainstorm that night. I'd had a couple of episodes like it before. When I was a kid, in fact. But, back then, someone would quickly cure me. Go out and play, don't be such a pain in the arse, stop bugging us with all your questions!

When people are always cutting you down, you don't get a chance to grow.

THE THIRD TIME I saw Margueritte, I arrived before her. I sat on the bench and scowled every time I saw a mother and her kids or some old guy with a walking stick heading in my direction. Pulling faces to scare passers-by so they would bugger off and find somewhere else.

This bench belonged to me and Margueritte. It was mine and hers, end of. The funniest thing was that I was waiting for her, my pigeon lady. And when I saw her at the far end of the path, tottering towards me on her skinny legs, wearing that flowery dress, the grey jacket, handbag dangling from the crook of her arm, it warmed my heart. Just like a kid of fifteen with his first girlfriend.

Well, not *just like*. But you know what I mean.

She gave me a little wave, wiggling her fingers, and I felt like laughing. And that's just it—if I had to explain what we have, her and me, that's how I'd describe it: a flicker of humour that makes you feel good. Happy.

She put down her bag and sat, carefully smoothing the creases in her dress. She said:

"Monsieur Chazes, what a pleasant surprise!"

"You can call me Germain, you know."

She smiled.

"Really? It would be a pleasure, Germain. But I shall do so only on the condition that you agree to call me Margueritte."

"Well… if you insist, I'd be happy to."

"I insist."

"OK, then, in that case…"

"Have you already counted our birds today?"

She had said "our birds", and I didn't find that strange. I said:

"I was waiting for you."

The worst thing is, it was true.

She frowned as though she was thinking about something important, then she said:

"Very well. So, tell me, Germain, how should we proceed? Would you like me to begin, so that you can do the recount? Shall we count aloud together? Would you rather we counted in silence and compared our results?"

"We each do it in our head," I said.

"Yes, you're quite right… I think in that way we are less likely to hinder or unduly influence each other. You have a scientific turn of mind, Germain. I like that."

And since she wasn't pulling my leg, I felt proud, and that's pretty rare.

We counted sixteen. I was able to introduce her to Fistfight, Little Grey, Klingon and two or three others she hadn't met before.

She had me repeat the last name, she didn't seem to know it.

"Klingon."

"Pardon?"

"You know, like the Klingons in *Star Trek*."

"No… no, I can't say I'm familiar with that particular cultural reference."

"Well, see, Klingons are aliens in *Star Trek*, but it can also mean an ankle biter, a little nipper, a crab. You know, cause they 'cling on'."

"A crab? Are you… ahem… are you referring to pubic lice?"

"No… well, yes, crab can mean that too, but a Klingon is a kid, a child… didn't you know?"

"Dear Lord no! Clearly I have much to learn from you."

"Yeah, because they cling on, they don't let go and they bug the hell out of you! And once you've got them, there's no getting rid, d'you see what I mean?"

"Ah, yes… I see… of course. Hence the parallel with *pthirus pubis*…"

"Exactly," I said. "Exactly like what you just said."

I wasn't too sure, but hey…

She giggled.

"Well, thanks to you, this will not have been a wasted day! I've learned something new."

"You're welcome. You scratch my back, I scratch yours."

She sat for a moment in silence and then suddenly, as if she'd remembered she'd left a saucepan on the stove, she said:

"Oh, I almost forgot…"

And she took a book out of her handbag and said:

"You know, Germain, I thought about you last night as I was rereading this novel."

"About *me?*"

I was completely shell-shocked.

"Oh yes, you. You and the pigeons. It came to me suddenly as I was reading a particular passage... Here, let me find it for you, wait a moment. Let's see... Ah, here it is: *How can one evoke, for example, a town without pigeons, without trees and without gardens, where one hears no beating of wings, no rustling of leaves, a non-place, in effect?*"

She stopped. She glanced at me, pleased as Punch, with the look of someone who has just given you a beautiful present. Me, I felt intimidated. I'm not used to people giving me sentences. Or thinking about me when they're reading books. I said:

"Could you say it again? Not so fast this time, if you don't mind..."

"Of course... *How can one evoke, for example, a town without pigeons, without trees and without gardens...*"

"That's there in the book?"

"Yes."

"It's a clever phrase. And it's true. A city without trees, without birds. What's the name of it, this book?"

"*The Plague*. The author's name is Albert Camus."

"My grandfather's name was Albert too. It's a weird title, *The Plague*. What's it about?"

"I can lend it to you, if you like..."

"Oh, you know, me and reading..."

She closed the book. She seemed to hesitate and then she said:

65

"Would you like me to read you a few passages? I enjoy reading aloud and I so rarely have the opportunity. As I'm sure you understand, if I started to read aloud sitting here alone on my bench, I think people might worry about my sanity…"

I said:

"You're absolutely right, they'd take you for a doddery old bat—no offence…"

She burst out laughing.

"Ha! Ha! A doddery old bat, that's precisely it! Which is a colourful way of saying a senile old fool… In any case, I simply wanted to suggest, if you are agreeable, I might read you a few select passages. You would be my pretext, you understand?… But I would not wish to bore you… It goes without saying that I shall read only if you would like me to. So, please, be honest: is it something you might enjoy?"

I said yes.

"Enjoy" was probably not exactly the word, but the prospect—*see also: eventuality, contingency*—was not exactly unpleasant.

I sometimes listen to stories on the radio, plays and stuff, while I'm whittling sculptures with my Opinel. And it's true that it keeps your ears busy.

M ARGUERITTE started to read, in her quiet, muffled voice. And then, maybe because she got caught up in the story, she started talking louder, and using different voices to let you know when there were different characters.

When you hear how brilliantly she does it, it doesn't matter how unwilling or uninterested you are, it's too late. You're trapped. Or at least I was, that first time—I was completely knocked for six.

She skipped the first two or three pages of the book, explaining:

"I think we should dive straight into the action, if that's all right with you."

And she added:

"I've always found preambles a little tedious… So… I need to set the scene a little: the story is set in Algeria, in a town called Oran…"

If she'd just said "in Oran", I would have had to pretend I knew where it was. But I knew about Algeria: Youss' had shown it to me on a map, because his parents were born there.

Anyway, she didn't even check to see whether I knew about geography or whatever. She calmly started reading, I didn't have to do anything.

"*On the morning of 16th April, Doctor Bernard Rieux came out of his consulting room and stumbled on a dead rat in the middle of the landing. At the time, he pushed the animal aside without a thought and went down the stairs. But once out on the street, the thought occurred to him that this rat…"*

As soon as she started reading, I knew I was going to like it. I didn't really know what sort of book it was, a horror story or a thriller, but it had grabbed me by the ears, the way you do with rabbits.

I could picture it, the dead rat. I could see it!

And the other one, the one scurrying down the corridor, half dead and spluttering blood. And later on, the doctor's wife when she's sick and in bed.

"… but by this time the townspeople had started to become concerned. Because from the 18th, hundreds of dying rats began to spill from the factories and the warehouses. In some cases, it was necessary to finish the creatures off, to put them out of their misery…"

Oh my God, it was brilliant! I could picture the dead critters everywhere, the whole town being overrun. It was like a movie, but just for me, inside my head. We were sitting in the middle of the park, the two of us, chilling out in the shade of the linden tree. And all around us, if I closed my eyes—and even if I didn't—there were huge piles of dead rats, swollen and stinking, their paws stiff. And everywhere there were others dying, whimpering, their pink tails wriggling.

"From nooks and basements, cellars and sewers, they scrabbled up in long shuddering lines and staggered into the light, there to reel and die…"

Ugh, it was disgusting, all these vermin! Just thinking about them gave me the shivers. If there's an animal that really turns my stomach, it's rats. Rats and cockroaches. Cockroaches make me want to puke.

Margueritte read a few pages, skipped a passage and carried on. I didn't say a word. I sat there wondering if the town's rat extermination service was going to deal with this shit or not. Because when you've seen the way they piss around in council offices… Well, in our town, in any case. Maybe things are different in Oran. I hope so, for their sake. Because if it happened round here, no offence, but we'd smother to death under piles of rats. And then, in the book, the concierge gets sick, and his glands are all swollen in his neck. I know all about swollen glands, because once I caught something and the glands in my groin swelled up so I know exactly how he felt. Especially because the bastard doctor pressed down on them hard.

When Margueritte stopped reading, I would have liked her to carry on. But since we weren't close friends, I didn't feel like I could ask. I just said:

"It's really interesting, your book."

She gave a little nod to let me know she agreed.

"Yes. Camus is certainly a great author."

"His first name is Albert, is that right? Albert Camus?"

"Indeed it is. Have you never read anything by him? *The Outsider? The Fall?*"

"I don't think so. Not that I remember, anyway."

"If you enjoyed my little reading, perhaps we could continue with the book another day if you're so inclined?"

I was so inclined I'd happily have carried on right now

this minute. At the same time, I wasn't about to spend my days sitting on park benches having someone read me stories like you do with little kids. Except that with kids, you don't read them stories about dead rats.

I said:

"Perhaps. Why not? I wouldn't mind."

Which is one way of saying yes without sounding too desperate.

We said goodbye without setting a date.

I walked with her a little way along the path. She headed for the gate onto the boulevard de la Libération. I prefer to leave by the avenue des Lices, it's shorter. Well, to get to where I'm going, it's shorter.

Everything is relative.

As I walked, I was thinking about what she had just been reading to me. Apart from the rats, there were other scenes I'd really liked. For example the neighbour who wants to commit suicide and writes in chalk on his door: *Come in, I've hanged myself.*

Come in, I've hanged myself! That just blows me away, you know? What must have been going on in this guy Camus's head to be able to come up with stuff like this!

Though I suppose sometimes, in real life... I remember, when I was a kid, one of our neighbours shot himself in the head. Lombard, his name was. He was afraid of his kids finding him when they came back from school, so he left a note on the front door too: *Gone shopping.* And so the dog wouldn't run away, he kept it locked inside with him. It was a huge grey-brown mutt, a vicious animal, a cross between a Wolfhound and a Great Dane. When the kids came home from school, they saw the note their dad had left and they heard the dog inside scratching at the door. They wanted to let it out, but the door was locked, so the boy told his sister to stay where she was and be good while he went round to the other side of the house and snuck in through a back window. He didn't come out again. When the mother came home from work and saw the note, and found her daughter alone on the front step and her son nowhere to be seen, she realized something wasn't right, the whole situation seemed sketchy.

She dropped her daughter round at ours and asked my mother to look after her. I remember being hacked off because she cried the whole time.

At first, we heard nothing. Then we heard the mother scream. Then the ambulance sirens. Then the police sirens. I went outside to find out what was going on, but I couldn't see anything much, just a bunch of people on the lawn crowding around a stretcher with a sheet over it.

Later, Madame Lombard told my mother that when she went into the house, she found her son standing, frozen in the kitchen, staring at the body of his father, which wasn't a pretty sight. Apparently the dog's muzzle was smeared with blood up to its ears. On the other hand, the floor was spotless, he'd licked the tiles clean. And his master's skull while he was about it. There was not a drop of blood, not a sliver of bone, not a lump of brain. It was perfect. Clean as a new pin.

I think the dog had to be put down or something.

It sent the wife completely off her rocker. From then on, any time she saw a dog in the street she'd shriek at the kids *Get over here! Quick! Quiiiick!* scaring them so much they nearly shat themselves.

Especially seeing as how the son was already pretty messed up by the experience.

Whereas if the father had simply written: *Come in, I've shot myself*, like Albert Camus, it would have spared the kid a nasty surprise.

But you can't always think of everything.

MARGUERITTE got through reading me *The Plague* in a couple of days. I mean, not all of it, obviously. Just extracts. And I have to say that mostly it was really good. With characters so completely twisted you had to wonder where Camus came up with them. The guy called Grand, for example, the one who wants to write a novel, except he writes the same sentence over and over, just changing a couple of words. It reminded me of *The Shining*, you know, the movie with Jack Nicholson, where the character types the same sentence hundreds of times on this battered old typewriter before he starts breaking down doors with an axe. There's another story that scared me witless. He's really good at playing psychos, Jack Nicholson.

Anyway, to get back to the book, one thing is certain, which is that the days Margueritte and I spent reading *The Plague*, time passed a lot quicker around the bench.

One day, she said to me:

"You're a true reader, Germain, I can tell…"

At the time, it made me laugh because, me and books, well, you know…

Thing is, she was serious. She told me that reading starts with listening. Me, I would have thought it started with reading. But she said: No, no, don't you believe it, Germain. To cultivate a love of reading in children, you have to read to them aloud. And she explained that if you did it properly, they were hooked, like it was a drug. Then, as they grow up, they need books. I was astonished, but, thinking about it I realized it made sense. If someone had read me stories as a kid, I might have spent more time reading books instead of getting myself in trouble because I was bored.

That's why the day she gave me the book I was really pleased, even if I was embarrassed too, because in my innermost self—*see also: in one's heart of hearts, deep inside*—I knew I would never read it, because it was too long and far too complicated.

She handed it to me, just like that, as she was getting up to leave, and she said:

"I've marked the passages we read together in pencil. Just as a reminder."

I said, OK, thanks. And I said it was kind of her. And told her I was happy.

She smiled.

"The pleasure was all mine, Germain, I assure you. Books should not be loved selfishly. Neither books nor anything else, in fact. We are here on this earth merely to pass things on… To learn to share our toys, that is perhaps the most important lesson to remember in this life… In fact, I was intending to introduce you to a number of other books I love, from time to time. Unless of course you are tired of listening to me… Would you like that?"

There are people you can't say no to. She was looking at me with her soft eyes, her gentle little wrinkly face, smiling at her own joke, as though she had just rung a doorbell and was about to leg it. I thought to myself that she must have driven quite a few men crazy in her day, just by asking what she'd asked me: "Would you like that?"

I just nodded. I felt happy but dumb; with me, the two often go together.

I watched her walk off down the path. I stood frozen, holding my book. It was my first book. I mean, the first book anyone had ever given me.

Since I didn't know what to do with it, I put it on top of the television when I got home. But that night, as I was about to turn off the TV and hit the sack, I looked at it. It was like it was waiting for me.

I heard that voice in my head again.

It was saying: *Oh for God's sake, Germain, at least make an effort! It's only a book.*

I picked it up, opened it, flicked past the first pages and looked for an underlined passage, and I found the sentence: *On the morning of 16th April, Doctor Bernard Rieux came out of his consulting room and stumbled on a dead rat in the middle of the landing.* And when I found it, it was easy enough to read, because I knew it already. To make it stand out better, I went over it with the highlighter pen I use for labelling the vegetables I sell down the market.

Then, I looked for: *Come in, I've hanged myself.* It took a while, but it was like a game. A treasure hunt. So I highlighted all the passages I really liked. Even today, *The Plague* is a book where I only read bits of pages. With other books—not counting the dictionary, which I don't read from cover to cover either—even if it's hard, even if I find it difficult, I keep going. Or at least I try.

But this one book... how can I explain it? I'll never read it all.

Because the version—*see also: interpretation*—that I like best is Margueritte's.

O NE DAY, not long after I was given *The Plague* as a present, I was at Chez Francine with Marco and Landremont. We were playing cards and watching the news. At some point, there was a report on some country, I don't really remember which one. Anyway, someplace where life pretty much sucked, what with wars and suchlike. This time, there had been an earthquake, a proper natural disaster with loads of people dead—according to early estimates by the foreign correspondent.

Landremont said:

"Jesus! Some people really have it rough, don't they? Those poor bastards have enough to deal with already. If it's not bombs raining from the sky, it's their roof caving in!"

Marco joined in:

"All they need now is a dose of cholera…"

"Or the plague, like in Oran in the book by Camus!" I said.

Landremont gave me a funny look. He opened his mouth but nothing came out, he turned to Marco and Julien, then back to me. And then he said, straight out:

"You're telling me you've read Camus?"

"Well… *The Plague*, that's all…"

"Really?… You've read *The Plague*, and 'that's all'? When did you start reading books?"

It got on my tits, the way he talked to me. I chugged my beer and, as I got up to leave, I said:

"I suppose you read a lot, do you?"

When I got outside, I thought, Next time you pull a stunt like that, you prick, I'll give you a slap.

Just to sort out his ideas, as my mother would say. And, seeing as how I was thinking about her, it occurred to me that I should pay her a visit one of these days while she was still alive.

M Y MOTHER lives thirty metres from my place. She lives in the house, I live in the garden. Well, in the caravan. That said, thinking about it, we couldn't be farther apart.

I suppose I could have looked for my own place, but what would be the point? I don't need much space, apart from a bed, a place to sit and somewhere to eat. I take up more than enough space as it is. People say that, given the size of me, a caravan must feel very small. But ever since I was a kid, I've always bumped into things, I've always been too big for my size. Annette says I'm magnificent. But since when can you trust the word of a woman in love? You know what they're like: they always think you're the strongest, the most handsome. Mothers can be a bit like that too, apparently. Those who are the maternal type, at least.

I stayed here on account of my vegetable garden. I created it all by myself. I turned over the soil with a spade—and that's no job for slackers, trust me. I built the fence with the little gate, the tool shed, the greenhouse. It's like my kid. Maybe that's a dumb thing to say. I don't care. Without me, it wouldn't exist. I grow a bit of everything: carrots, turnips, beetroot, potatoes, leeks. Different types of lettuce: frisée, romaine, some Batavian. Tomatoes too, beefsteak and Black Krim, as well as Marmandes. Anyhow, it depends on the season and on how I feel. And I plant flowers too, just for show. I was young when I started it. I don't quite remember how old—twelve, maybe thirteen?

My mother screamed at me like a fishwife, saying I'd turned her lawn into a building site. "Lawn"? You must be kidding. A patch of wilderness, more like.

These days, she doesn't say anything. But she comes down and steals my vegetables as soon as my back is turned. In the beginning, I'd bawl her out, but actually, I don't really care. I've got ten times as many vegetables as I can use. Sometimes I even go down the market and sell them. And besides, at least trekking down the garden and back with her basket gives my mother a bit of exercise. She could do with it, she barks like a seal when she breathes, her lungs will be the death of her, or maybe her heart. One or the other. Her mind is gone already. But being brain-dead isn't fatal: even when your mind is gone, you can live on. Too bad for those around you.

The day I told my mother I was going to move into the caravan at the bottom of the garden, she looked at me like I was soft in the head. She said:

"Can't you think of a better way to make us look bad to the neighbours?"

I replied, keeping my cool:

"I don't give a damn about the neighbours! And I can't see why they would be bothered. It's our garden…"

She collapsed on the sofa. She was panting hard, one hand on her chest.

"God Almighty, what did I ever do to deserve a son like this?"

"To God Almighty? Nothing." I said.

"Oh, go away! You make me tired. Go and live in that caravan of yours for all I care!"

I walked out and left her, I didn't respond, I didn't even turn back.

I LIKE THIS CARAVAN. I resprayed it white and built an arbour over it to train a vine. It keeps me cool in summer and acts as a gutter during the rainy season. The caravan doesn't belong to me, but I don't think there's any danger of the owner coming to claim it. Not if he values his balls, at any rate.

Gardini, his name is. Jean-Michel Gardini.

He showed up at the house one day. I was still a kid at the time, nine or ten maybe. Not much older. I do know I hadn't started on my vegetable garden yet and that I was still going to school more or less. That gives me a couple of reference points.

This guy showed up one morning and asked my mother if he could park his caravan on our land because he was here for two weeks "on business".

I don't know about you, but a guy who sleeps in an Eriba Puck and comes around telling you he's "on business" makes me suspicious. Well, it would make me suspicious now, but back then nothing seemed strange or surprising because I was still a kid.

In fact his "business", we found out later, was selling knock-off jewellery at local markets.

Anyway, there he was explaining to my mother that someone down at the town hall had mentioned we had a large garden and that he'd like to rent part of it while he was here. And, while they were on the subject, he was prepared to pay extra if she would cook lunch for him every day.

At the time, my mother was pretty much living from hand to mouth. She did a few little jobs here and there, but nothing out of the ordinary. So the prospect of renting out a bit of waste ground that no one ever used—except me as a playground, but I didn't count—of taking in a lodger, half-board, cash in hand, no word to the taxman, gave her pause for thought. Though it wasn't a long pause.

I think she'd said yes before he finished his sentence.

I hated this Gardini from the moment I set eyes on him, the two-faced fucker. He was a flash bastard, all tailored suits and stripy shirts. He wore his hair down over his shoulders, leaving snowdrifts of dandruff. He was trying his best to look artistic, but really he was just an arsehole, something I knew all about even then. Just having to sit opposite him at breakfast, lunch and dinner was too much for me. The way he ate was disgusting. He never washed his hands when he came out of the toilet, but that didn't stop him helping himself to bread from the basket. He was forever talking with his mouth full, and I would spend the whole meal calculating the trajectories—*line (parabola) describing the path followed by a projectile after launch*—to avoid ending up with breadcrumbs floating in my water glass.

My mother would yell at me:

"Germain, what's got into you? You're holding on to that glass for dear life. Would you ever just put it down! No one's going to steal it! Children, I tell you… You wouldn't believe what I have to put up with, Monsieur Gardini!"

"Call me Jean-Mi, Madame Chazes. All my friends call me Jean-Mi."

"I couldn't possibly…"

"Even if I ask nicely?"

"Well… as long as you call me Jacqueline. Germain, you'll get a slap if you're not careful."

"Jacqueline? Such a charming name. It suits you… You must be so proud to be blessed with such an elegant name."

"That's so true."

This was news to me. She spent her time moaning to her girlfriends:

"Jacqueline makes me sound like an old biddy. I prefer Jackie…" And Gardini, bowing and scraping to get into her good books, telling her how she cooked like a queen, how she deserved a Michelin star. How she was one of the ten wonders of the world. He had a good line in soft soap… Long story short, after a couple of days they hardly even talked during meals, they were so busy devouring each other with their eyes. At first, I was happy, I didn't have to play goalie with my water glass any more. But even though I was a kid, I wasn't completely blind. Whenever my mother got up from the table to get more bread or fill the water jug, I noticed that Gardini watched her like a stray dog watching someone take away its bowl. And that he mostly stared at her below the waterline.

Sometimes, after the cheese course, he'd start jiggling on his seat like a corn kernel on a hotplate. Then he'd say:

"I've brought some lovely stuff back from my studio in Paris. Would you like me to show you?"

"It would be a pleasure, but you do know I couldn't possibly afford—"

"I'd just like you to see them."

And my mother would say:

"Well, in that case…"

Gardini sprinted down to the end of the garden and came back with the large briefcase stamped *Brotard & Gardini—Authentic Parisian Chic—Jewellery and Finery* that he always kept in the boot of his Simca.

In the meantime, my mother would have cleared away the plates. Gardini would set the case on the table. He would start giving her the sales pitch while he showed her his tacky crap.

"Here, try on this necklace. It's genuine silver plate, look at the hallmark! Go on, try it on! Just for me… It would beautifully show off that elegant neck of yours."

I wondered why he was always talking about her neck since the necklaces were never chokers, but chains that dangled down to her breasts.

Gardini was always helpful, I'll say that for him. He would go round behind her and press up against her.

"Just a minute, Jacqueline, just a minute, I'll put it on for you."

It must have been a tricky process, because he seemed to struggle for a long time behind her. My mother would giggle loudly. He would blush and his voice sounded hoarse.

Eventually, my mother would say:

"Germain, I've just noticed the time, shouldn't you get back to school?"

That was suspicious in itself since usually she didn't give a shit whether I went to school or not. Then she'd say, in this strange, soft voice:

"Go on, go on, you don't want to be late."

And I thought to myself, women are stupid, one silly necklace and suddenly they're in a good mood.

Kids are so dumb.

GARDINI WAS QUICK to get his feet under the table. He would come for two weeks, disappear for three days, then come back again, and so on. He would stretch his size 11s farther and farther under the table, sink deeper and deeper into the sofa. He had decided to, as he put it, take me in hand.

He started giving me orders, Tidy your room, set the table, stop bugging me, go to bed. He started calling my mother by her first name and finding fault while he was at it, You've put too much salt in the stew, fetch me a can of beer, what's keeping you with the coffee?

My mother may be a fine filly, but don't go jerking the reins. In our family, we've got short fuses. I don't know if I told you: I get my height from her. Obviously her height is a bit more feminine. But not much more, relatively speaking. Gardini just about came up to her ear.

Anyway, what is bound to happen, happens. That's the law of fate, and I've noticed that it's a law that also means shit happens.

One night, I don't really remember why, he gave me a clout. Now, my mother might not have had an ounce of maternal fibre, but she had a sense of propriety. Only one person was allowed to wallop her son and that was her. She said:

"I won't have you hit that child!"

"Shut your hole!" Gardini said.

"What?" my mother said, "What did you just say to me?"

"You heard me! And stop busting my balls, I'm watching the match."

My mother turned off the TV. Gardini roared:

"Turn the fucking TV back on!"

"No," said my mother.

Gardini lost his head, he leapt to his feet and said: "Jesus H. Christ! You're asking for a slap too!"

He lashed out at my mother, whack whack, and gave her a box round the ears. Now that, that was a mistake.

My mother went completely white, she walked out without a word, she went straight to the garage.

She came back with a pitchfork. And my mother waving a pitchfork is not something you laugh at. Especially when she's pointing it at your belly and saying in a patient voice:

"You're packing up your bags and you're leaving."

Gardini tried to come on like gangbusters. He stepped towards her, raising his hand, really threatening as if to say, What, you want a second helping, haven't you had enough?

My mother stabbed him—*tchak*—right in his blubbery thigh. A quick, fast jab, like a torero in a bullfight. The guy started bleeding and screaming:

"Ow-shit-fuck-shit! You're a bloody lunatic!"

My mother said:

"Looks that way."

Then she added:

"I'm going to count to three. One…"

Gardini grabbed the keys to the Simca off the sideboard, stumbled backwards towards the door, saying:

"Think about it, Jacqueline, think carefully! If I walk out this door, you'll never see me again!"

"I've already thought about it. Two…"

"I forgive you!"

My mother lifted the pitchfork, aiming an inch or two higher. She said:

"Three."

Gardini said Ow-fuck-shit-fuck! a couple more times—varying the order—then legged it down the garden.

He climbed behind the wheel of his car, waved his fist, screaming, This isn't the end of it! and took off at top speed leaving the caravan behind since, that particular morning, it was unhitched.

A few days later, Monsieur Saunier—he was mayor at the time—came by to see my mother.

"Listen, the reason I've come to see you is because we've had a call at the office from a man named Gardini about a caravan that is apparently parked on your property."

"That's true."

"He wants it back."

"Let him come round," my mother said, "I'll give him a warm welcome."

"You sound hostile, Jackie," said the mayor, "Do you have some grievance against this man?"

My mother said:

"He's been beating my lad."

"Oh…" said the mayor.

"And me."

"Really?"

"What are you planning to do? Send the police round?"

"And why would I do that?… You've assured me that, if he should show his face, the gentleman will get a warm welcome, haven't you?"

"That's what I said."

"You have not made any threats against him in my presence, have you?"

"No."

"In that case, it is a personal matter that does not concern the local police. You have every right to give a friend a *warm welcome*."

"Damn right," my mother said, "It's a free country!"

"In that case, I believe we're done. Oh, no, while I think of it… I don't suppose you have a pitchfork by any chance?"

"In the garage."

"Would you lend it to me for… let's say two or three months?"

The chicken-shit bastard phoned to threaten my mother every night for a few weeks. Then the calls became less frequent. Eventually they stopped.

"But Jackie, what will you do if he comes back?" the neighbours would ask.

And my mother would say:

"A mischief."

She always was a woman of few words.

IN THE BEGINNING, I used the caravan as a playhouse, later as a shag pad, and it was really practical. Eventually, one day, I decided to make it my primary residence.

It has to be said that my mother was getting to be unbearable.

She was getting to be completely batshit crazy, which was sad since she was only sixty-three. She'd got to where she only talked to the cat, and even then it was just repeating the same old things. She wasn't interested in anything any more except her magazines; she would spend all day cutting out photos of American actors and pasting them over photos in the family albums. I don't have much in the way of memories, and I don't really give a toss, but it scared the crap out of me—to put it politely—seeing Tom Cruise or Robert De Niro pasted over my grandfather or my uncle Georges.

When I asked her why she was doing it, she said:

"I'm tired of looking at his ugly mug."

"Are you talking about Grandad or Uncle Georges?"

"Both. They're as bad as each other."

I came to the point where I thought that with parents, the only thing is to get out as early as you can. I hope the Good Lord can forgive such ingratitude, but He had it easy, His mother was a saint. So He can't really compare the two.

I'm talking about normal people, crazy people like my old lady.

You don't get this sort of problem with animals. When sparrows leave the nest, they don't come back for lunch every Sunday as far as I know. And their parents don't go round saying, What sort of time do you call this? Where have you been? Wipe your feet before you come in! Beasts are cleverer than us, even if they are dumb animals.

Obviously, it was down to me to move out, to leave my mother. But seeing as how her health wasn't too good, I hung around a bit longer. In case the house became vacant. And besides, like I told you, I had the vegetable garden to think about. And if you haven't experienced it, let me tell you: a garden has a greater hold on you than a scraggy bit of umbilical cord. If I'm allowed to say such a thing about something that is a family tie—and therefore sacred—I hope God won't chalk it up on my slate.

Then again, Julien is always saying: "No matter what you do, Germain, she'll always be your mother. In this life, we only get one mother. You'll see, when she's gone, you'll be the first to shed a tear."

And that really hacks me off. Me, shed tears for my mother? Over my dead body, I thought. All she ever did was bring me into this world, and then only because she couldn't get rid of me, because once I was inside her I had to come out somehow. And I'm supposed to cry for her?

Where's the justice in that?

*

These days, I know that it's not possible to explain everything.

Emotions, for example, are often irrational—*see also: unreasonable, unwarranted, senseless*. My mother was like a stone in my shoe. Something that isn't really serious, but still manages to ruin your life.

So, one day, I decided to leave home. The last straw was when I saw her on her own in the kitchen screaming at the ants because they were leaving footprints all over the sink.

That was the point when I thought, right, now she really has gone too far.

Let her die, I thought, I don't care, this time, I'm definitely out of here.

It came to me like a sudden urge, like when you desperately need to take a leak, with much the same result—a huge feeling of relief once it's done.

That night I talked to my friends down at the bar. I was happy. I said:

"I've left home."

Landremont threw his hands up to heaven and said:

"Praise Jesus! It's a miracle! So you've finally made up your mind?"

"Yeah, it's done and dusted."

"So where are you going to sleep?"

"In the caravan."

"In the caravan?" Julien repeated. "Yeah… it's not a bad idea, I suppose. I didn't realize it was still roadworthy… So where are you planning to park it? At the camp site?"

"I'm not planning to park it anywhere, I'm leaving it where it is."

Jojo laughed and Landremont buried his head in his hands.

Julien said:

"Oh… Let me get this right, you're saying that you've left home and moved to the bottom of the garden, is that it?"

"Yeah, why?"

Julien shook his head slowly. Marco said:

"He's a certified bona fide grown-up now, our Germain."

Landremont sniggered. He said:

"Certified, I'm not sure; *certifiable*, definitely."

Everyone laughed, especially me. That's what I always do when I don't get the joke. But to be honest, I thought about it that night while I was cooking some grub, and I still couldn't see what the wankers were laughing at. What was the problem with me leaving home and moving into the Eriba Puck? Distance is all in your head. Moving to the bottom of the garden was *symbolic*, so to speak. That's what I would have told them if I'd had the word handy at the time. That's exactly what I would have said.

The caravan was symbolic.

And besides, being nearby, it was practical.

ONE TIME—I can't quite remember why—Margueritte asked me:

"Have you still got your mother, Germain?"

"Oh yes, still…" I said.

I could have added "Worse luck!" but I figured that Margueritte probably wouldn't understand that kind of thing. Especially since, right then, she heaved a big sigh.

"Oh, you are so lucky."

What could I possibly say to that?

Given her age, Margueritte probably lost hers long ago. I thought maybe she still misses her. Maybe old people feel like orphans too, when they lose their mother.

It must have been something like that, because she decided we were going to start another book "that beautifully describes a mother's love. You'll see, it is terribly moving…"

Promise at Dawn, it's called.

At first I didn't really understand all the stories of gods with strange names. Totoche and I don't know who all. A bit later, I really got into it, when the hero talks about how he found his vocation when he was thirteen, except for him it wasn't rose windows, it was wanting to be a writer, but as jobs go, it's no stupider than any other.

Margueritte read a bit to me.

I said, It's not bad for a made-up story.

She shook her head and said:

"Actually, it's autobiographical!"

"That's what I said."

"In other words, the author is writing about his own childhood, his real mother, about himself, about being a pilot during the war. He is telling the story of his life."

"Really?"

"Oh yes, I assure you. He is describing what he experienced, what he felt…"

"Even when he talks about howling like a dog over the grave?"

"Like a dog?… I'm not sure what—ah, yes, I think I remember. Indeed, I think he may have used those very words. Just a moment, just a moment, let me check…"

She flicked the pages with the edge of her thumb— *zzzzip*—like a dealer shuffling a pack of cards.

I was thinking, she's showing off, no one can read that fast without even opening the book the whole way. But apparently they can, because suddenly she screeched to a halt and said:

"Ah, I've found it! *You constantly return to howl at your mother's grave like a lost dog.* Well, well, Germain, I'm impressed, you have excellent auditory memory."

"Well, actually, I mostly remember things that I hear…"

She began rereading the passage silently, selfishly. I said:

"Couldn't you read it out loud?"

"I would be happy to! All the more so as it is so poignant, listen: *It is not good to be so loved so young, so early. It leaves you with a fatal flaw. You believe that love is possible. You believe that it exists elsewhere, that it can be found. You stake your life on it. You watch, you hope, you wait. Through a mother's love, life makes a promise at dawn that it can never keep… And so, to the end of your days, you are destined to be disenchanted."*

"So that's where it comes from, the title?"

"Hmm?"

"The writer called it *Promise at Dawn* because life makes promises that it doesn't keep? It's about a mother's love."

"Of course, absolutely! It's astonishing to realize that I never noticed that crucial detail in all the times I read it!"

"Could you keep going a little bit, just as far as the dog?"

"As far as the end of the chapter would be even better."

"OK."

"Thereafter, each time a woman takes you in her arms and clasps you to her breast, it is merely a condolence. You constantly return to howl at your mother's grave like a lost dog."

"There: 'like a lost dog', see!"

"… Never again, never again, never again. Beautiful arms twine about your neck, the softest lips speak to you of love, but already you know the score. You have drunk from the source early and slaked your thirst. When, later, you grow thirsty, though you search high and low, you will find there are no more springs, only mirages."

"Does he say that because he was a pilot?"

"Say what?"

"You did tell me he was a pilot, the guy who wrote this?"

"Yes, yes absolutely."

"So, it's because he was a pilot that he mentions Mirages in the story?"

You'd think I was speaking Chinese.

"I'm sorry, Germain, I'm not quite sure what you're saying…"

"I was saying that a Mirage is a type of fighter plane."

"Is it? I didn't know that."

"I suppose even you can't know everything."

"Very true. And it's fortunate, for otherwise I should be terribly bored. That said, in the novel, I believe the author is using the word *mirage* in a different sense. Its other meaning, if you prefer. A mirage is an optical illusion. You know the sort of thing, when you think you can see pools of water on the road when it's hot in summer."

"Oh, yes, of course, now you mention it… I knew that."

"This is why, on the subject of love, Romain Gary writes: *there are no more springs, only mirages…* You think it is love, but in fact it is not. It is only an illusion."

"That's a figure of speech, isn't it?"

She set the book down on her lap and said:

"Yes, exactly, it's a figure of speech. It's what's known as a metaphor."

"A me-ta-for?"

"Yes, a metaphor. An image, if you prefer…"

Then she brought a finger to her lips and whispered *shh!* with a smile, then she carried on reading.

"*I am not saying that mothers should be forbidden from loving their children. I am simply saying that it is best that mothers have someone other they can love. If my mother had had a lover, I would not have spent my life languishing and thirsting next to every spring. Unfortunately for me, I know how to recognize a true diamond.*"

I thought to myself that Monsieur Gary and I had had very different life experiences, even if we had at least two things in common: a father who'd gone AWOL and a mother who smoked a bit too much.

I also thought he was laying it on a bit thick. No one could love their mother as much as he claims.

Margueritte had a faraway look in her eyes, she seemed happy. She whispered softly: *there are no more springs, only mirages…*

"What if it's the other way round?" I said.

Margueritte raised an eyebrow.

"The other way round?"

"What if the spring had dried up, what if there was no well. Well, you know what I mean…"

"You mean what if one was not loved as a child?"

"Supposing. What would happen?"

She thought for a moment. Then she said:

"Well, if you… I mean if someone did not receive enough love as a child, one might say that they have everything still to discover."

"So, actually, it would be better. Because I have to say, Gary sounds really dismissive, the way he talks about women. All that stuff about the dog howling over the grave… You don't think that maybe the guy was a depressive?"

"He committed suicide…"

"Well, there you go, then. That's what I was saying. I think that if his mother had brought him up the hard way, it would never have come to that."

"Was your mother strict?"

"Mine? She didn't care one way or the other."

Margueritte put away her book, she sighed, she said:

"I feel sorry for you. There is nothing worse than indifference. Especially from a mother."

"Well, what can you do? She didn't have the fibre."

MARGUERITTE never had kids. It's a pity, because I think they would have turned out well, with a mother like her teaching them culture in between juggling test tubes and reading them Camus—and leaving out the boring bits. Problem is, they were never born, so they never got to find out what they missed. For me vice is versa, if you know what I mean. I was born into this world by accident and I stayed out of habit.

People shouldn't have children if they've got no use for them. Because a kid puts more demands on your life than a dog in terms of responsibilities. And you can't just leave it by the side of the road, unless you want to wind up behind bars, but I'm sure you worked out that that was just a figure of speech.

But the thing is, meeting Margueritte and talking to her about life made me see my mother in a different light. I didn't suddenly love her, that would be pushing things a bit far! But I felt sorry for her. As a human being, I mean. Because her and me, we spent our whole lives screaming at each other—well, she did most of the screaming—and punching holes in the walls—that bit was mostly me. But she's still my mother. Julien is right, though it pisses me off to admit it. She didn't have me deliberately, obviously. She got pregnant with me the same way those Algerians got the plague. I'm an accident, a mistake. That said, she could have loved me anyway. It's been known. Take Julien, for example. When he talks about David, his eldest boy, he always says:

"My son was an unintended side-effect of a particularly boozy night out."

But you should see him with his kid, he loves the bones of him.

If I don't have a kid, it's probably for the best. Well, in a manner of speaking. I think I would have liked to have a kid. Sometimes when I look at Annette, I think how beautiful she'd look if she was pregnant. And even more beautiful with a baby in her arms. My baby, I mean. Thing is, what could I give a kid? Not much of a prize, a father like me, with no qualifications. A guy who'd never read a book in his life before the age of forty-five and even then only bits of *The Plague* by Albert Camus. A sad loser who can't even string three fucking words together without effing and blinding.

Apart from taking him fishing and showing him how to whittle, taking advantage of the knots and the grain of the wood, I'd have nothing to teach him. I wouldn't be a good role model. I wouldn't know how to bring him up.

That said, Annette would really like me to get her up the duff, I know that. Sometimes, when we're in bed, she takes my hand, lays it on her belly and whispers in my ear:

"How about we make one tonight?"

And feeling her next to me, so silky and warm, soft as a pillow, I'd give her ten kids and I know I'd love every one.

ANNETTE, she had a kid once. She lost the baby, some stupid illness, I don't really know the details. She never talks about it. Even though I'm a man, I think I can understand what it's like for a woman, losing a baby. Ever since, she's been bursting at the seams with tears, she's lumbered with all this love and she has no outlet for it. Maybe that's why she's so beautiful. Sometimes sadness tans your hide so deeply that afterwards you're soft and silky. My mother is a perfect example of the reverse: tough as old boots, silky as sixty-grit sandpaper.

It's true: life didn't do her any favours. She carried me like a burden, and as soon as she started to show she was thrown out and called a slut. Seems like her mother obviously didn't have much in the way of maternal fibre either.

Maybe the love between a mother and child is part of heredity—*The set of characteristics and traits inherited from one's parents*—to use one of Margueritte's words when she talks about science. Loving just wasn't one of my mother's traits.

I remember what she used to tell the neighbours about my birth when I was a kid.

"Ten hours it took. Ten hours of suffering worse than a dumb animal. He refused to come out, he was so big. Five kilos, can you imagine? Five kilos! Just think what that does to you. I'll tell you: it's like I took these two litres of milk, a bag of sugar, a kilo of flour and a packet of butter and,

104

I don't know, those onions over there. Five kilos! They had to drag him out with a forceps and I had to have stitches. So after that, I said to myself, I said, never again! Especially given all the satisfaction you get, when you realize how much trouble they are…"

When I heard her telling the story, I'd feel guilty. I'd look at all the food on the table, the milk, the sugar, the onions, a whole basketful of groceries, and it would go round and round in my head: five kilos, five kilos, five kilos…

I wished I could shrivel up and disappear.

But it was like it was deliberate; the more I tried to make myself smaller, the more every bit of me seemed determined to grow. My feet, especially. God, how my mother used to rant and rave about having to buy me new shoes every three months.

"Have you any idea how much you cost me? Keep this up and you can go to school in your bare feet. In your bare feet, I'm not joking."

It's not that I didn't want to curl up my toes like olden-day Chinese women—I saw a documentary about them once—but it's really painful, wearing shoes that are too tight. And besides, sooner or later they would wear out. And one morning, there would be a hole in the sole right under my big toe, or the whole seam would split.

My mother would start yelling about how she told me so! How she couldn't believe it, a new pair of shoes she'd only just bought me. How I was doing it on purpose. How all I was good for was making her life a misery. Nothing else.

Then she would sigh and examine the shoes from every angle and when she was completely convinced that I couldn't go on wearing them, she would drag me to the Shoe Palace. She would barge into the shop, shouting at the top of her voice to drown out the door chime: "Monsieur Bourdelle!"

And the short-arse at the back of the shop behind his bead curtain would yell back:

"Coming, Commming! Just a second!"

He would burst out of the back room and bear down on me hungrily. He looked like a fat spider about to gobble a fly. I couldn't stand the guy.

He would take off my shoes instead of letting me do it myself. He sweated like a pig, his hands were clammy and he'd grope my feet and say:

"Oh, he's got big feet! Very big feet! Let's see, let's see... 39, 40? Yessss, 40 it is. He's a big lad for his age. If he keeps growing like this, he'll have to have shoes made to measure!"

I would have punched him if I'd been big enough. But at ten years old, it wasn't a possibility. And later, when I could have decked him, it wasn't really relevant. With men, growing older sometimes cools down the thirst for revenge, not like elephants.

My mother always picked the cheapest, ugliest shoes.

"Give him something solid, Monsieur Bourdelle, something he might get a bit of wear out of this time."

And Bourdelle would wipe the sweat from his forehead and say: "Funny you should say that, Madame Chazes, I've just had something in I think you'll like! A new model that offers excellent ankle support. Snug fitting, crepe soles, and if that's not enough, they're Italian!"

"Oh, well," my mother would say, "If they're Italian, I'll take them. But you know with *this one*, nothing ever lasts."

This one was me.

Bourdelle would rummage through his unsold stock and then come back all fake smile and tell me I was in luck, that they had only one pair left in my size.

"You'll see, they'll last. See how stylish they are? Young people love them, they're very sporty."

From a grey or brown shoebox, he would take out a pair of shit-kickers, the sort of clodhoppers a country priest might wear. He would try to force them on, saying:

"Don't tense your foot, push down with your heel. Thaaat's it, lad. You see? I told you he was a size forty."

My mother would say:

"Let me have a look."

She would frown and give him a tight-lipped stare, then nod to let him know she wasn't born yesterday. In the end, she would always say:

"Tell you what, give him one size bigger, that should give me a bit of leeway."

And so I would leave with shoes too big for me that I had to wear until they fell apart.

It's funny the things you remember about your childhood. The shoes that were so huge they rubbed my feet raw only to crush my toes later and leave me with blisters. That, and the trousers so short you could see my ankles and my friends would take the piss:

"Hey, Chazes, you're at half mast! Did somebody die?"

Then there was the monthly trip to Chez Mireille, the salon where my mother had her hair dyed and old ladies went to get perms. I felt mortified just stepping through the door. The other boys all went to Monsieur Mesnard, the barber who cut their fathers' hair. But since I didn't have a father, I had to make do with a cut and blow job from a hairstylist—and unfortunately, that's a figure of speech.

I was always given the chair next to the window. I used to feel like the whole village traipsed past whenever I was there. That everyone would see me with my feet dangling in the air, my wet hair plastered to my skull and neatly parted in the middle. The assistant would put a pink towel around my shoulders. She would press her huge breasts against my back, so that was one good thing about it.

Then she would cut my hair with scissors instead of clippers like the other boys in my class. The haircut was probably fine, but every time I left the salon there was someone calling me names. People say names will never hurt you. But they're wrong, names hurt just as much as sticks and stones. They just break your bones more slowly.

Obviously, I wasn't the only badly dressed kid in my class. But, in case you hadn't noticed, other people's troubles are no consolation when you've got your own. It's not even as though it makes you feel you're not so alone. Sometimes, it's the opposite.

Landremont, who's got a thing for proverbs, always says: That which doesn't kill you makes you stronger.

So that's life, then, you're either strong or dead?

Talk about a shitty choice.

MY MOTHER AND ME, we don't talk much. We give each other a wide berth. From time to time, I have a look to see if the back door is open, if she's got washing on the line. Otherwise, I don't need to see her to know what she's up to. I can imagine. At eight o'clock every morning she comes downstairs in her dressing gown and slippers. She makes herself coffee—no sugar—and eats the last of yesterday's bread slathered with butter while she watches some soap opera on TV. She washes the breakfast dishes and then goes upstairs to put on her face. When she comes down again, she's wearing mascara, lipstick and perfume. My mother likes perfume. She always wears it, but not too much. It's still possible to breathe. It would embarrass me if she was tarty. She is my mother, after all. In front of the mirror in the hall she fixes her hair and says, Well, well, old girl, or, Would you look at the state of me this morning! and she sighs. Then she goes out to do her shopping.

She's sixty-three but she doesn't look it. She looks older. It's loneliness that does that. And maybe the two packs of smokes she gets through every day. I wouldn't mind, but she knows perfectly well that Smoking Kills, like they say in the warnings on the packets she chucks away.

Coming back from the shop is a 500-metre climb. When she gets back, she's out of breath.

When I was a kid, I'd sometimes say:

"You shouldn't smoke, Maman."

And she'd say:

"You suck the life out of me faster than the ciggies, so don't go lecturing me. And don't call me Maman, you know it annoys me."

And I'd say:

"Yes, Maman."

She always thought I was doing it to wind her up. But I was never able to call her Jacqueline or Jackie. I tried my best, but I just couldn't. It was Maman or nothing.

And nothing wasn't an option.

T HERE WERE BIG changes at Francine's. With Francine, not the restaurant.

I showed up one night at about seven. She was on her own, cleaning glasses behind the bar. I put both hands on the zinc counter and leaned over to kiss her cheek. I said:

"Hi! All right?"

I could tell it was the wrong question, because up close it was obvious that Francine was anything but all right. She had a red nose and eyes to match.

I rephrased and started over:

"Hi! Not good?"

"Not great…" she said in a tiny voice.

"You're not sick?"

She shook her head, No, no.

"So what's the matter? You look like someone died…"

She burst into tears and rushed into the back room.

I was completely discombobulated—*see also: disconcerted*— you could have knocked me down with a feather.

Jojo came out of the kitchen waving at me to shut up.

I whispered:

"What's going on?"

"Youssef is gone."

"Gone where?"

"What do I know? He's gone, that's all there is to it. There was a row yesterday when they were closing up. Turns out he's seeing someone else. Francine isn't taking it too well, so best not to rub salt in the wound, you understand?"

I understood perfectly, especially since we've spent the past three years taking bets on how long they would last. Francine still looks good, for her age. Problem is, that means she could have been his mother if she'd started young. She's got sixteen years on him, imagine! And she's jealous with it. She couldn't stand another girl so much as looking at her man sideways.

Now, Youssef's not the kind to bang anything that moves, but it's only human for a man to have close encounters of a sexual kind. As long as it's hygienic, I'm not about to cast the first stone.

Jojo added:

"This is just between us, so you have to keep it to yourself, OK? The girl he's banging is Stéphanie."

I said, Oh, shit!

He said: Yeah, but shh!

Stéphanie's just a kid—she's eighteen, maybe not even that. Francine has her help out behind the bar sometimes when the place is rammed. I'm not saying it's her own fault.

When Francine came back, snuffling, I comforted her as best I could.

"Give it time, he'll get tired of Stéphanie, you'll see. Youss' is the stay-at-home type, he's a creature of habit. Besides, he knows the best wine comes in old bottles."

Francine looked at me like she couldn't believe what I'd just said, then wailed and ran out sobbing.

Jojo threw his arms wide and said:

"Jesus, you're really amazing, you know that."

I said:

"Don't mention it, just trying to help."

Later, I reassured Francine. I explained that even if the bodywork had seen better days, it was her inner beauty that mattered. As an example I told her about Monsieur Massillon and his black 1956 Simca Versailles, and how, even though it looked like a Sherman tank and some people laughed at him, he'd had an offer of €7,000 for the old wreck, so there!

Francine sobbed some more.

Women are like that, they need to pour their hearts out. In the end I left her with Jojo because the situation was getting to be awkward: every time I said something to cheer her up, it started her off again. Some people just can't help it, they don't know how to accept sympathy.

Jojo said, Don't come back for a bit, yeah, give her a chance to calm down…

I told him not to worry, because I had shopping to do.

"Good, fine, you go do your shopping. And take your time about it."

I left him to deal with Francine. The whole story had left me brooding and thinking and stuff.

In a way, other people's troubles are useful. You realize how lucky you are not to have the same problems as them and you freak out when you think that it could have been you.

In this case, I was thinking that even though this had nothing to do with me, one day Annette and me would end up in the same situation. She's thirty-six, I'm forty-five. Sooner or later we'll be out of sync.

I headed off to Super U with this thought stuck in my throat.

ANNETTE AND ME, we never arrange to meet up, we don't need to. Sometimes she's there when I call round, sometimes she's not. And it's the same for me. We're free agents.

Freedom is something I value a lot, even if I don't really know what to do with it.

I'm very attached to my autonomy. Especially when it comes to my relations with women—and when I use the word *relation* I obviously mean it in the sense of *relations between two people*, but also, specifically (*in a stricter sense*): *sexual relations*. For a long time, I found women really annoying, always wanting to conduct a survey after sex when all you want to do is say nothing.

"Do you love me? Do you think about me a lot? What do you think when you think about me? Do you miss me when I'm not around?"

It has to be said that I couldn't really see the difference between loving someone and getting my leg over. What more proof of love could they want when I'd just given them my best?

"Do you love me?" was the one that really left me speech-less. As you know, I'm pretty leery about words. *Love* is a very intense word, it takes some getting used to. If someone has said it to you every day since you were a kid, I'm sure it's easier to come out with. But if no one said it to you until you were the wrong side of forty, it's difficult to get the word out, it gets stuck.

Women in general, as I'm sure you've noticed, are not the same as us. Their idea of love is clingy; whereas for men a cuddle is like a pair of handcuffs that makes them—well, me, in any case—want to get the hell out, pronto. That's one of the reasons I appreciate Annette. She loves me, which is already a point in her favour given that I'm not exactly the type of guy who inspires passion. And she doesn't expect me to be vice versa—*see also: reciprocal, mutual.*

We've got no problems with reciprocality, her and me.

One day, she said to me:

"I'm really lucky that you exist."

I said:

"Why?"

She said:

"Because I love you."

What was I supposed to do?

There was a time I would have laughed it off. I would have joked about it with my mates in the bar. But the day she said it, I'd just started all my contemplations on life and everything else. I had felt new feelings and emotions, especially when she and I were making love. So I listened to her and I didn't say anything. I didn't laugh at all. I think I was starting to understand the difference between sex and love, to put it politely. And, incidentally, for anyone who hasn't had the experience, it's easy to spot: when you love, things are not as funny. In fact they're serious. You think about the other person and it makes you go all funny and you think, Oh, fuck!

And it scares the shit out of you, believe me.

I should have cottoned on earlier when I started thinking the words "make love" to myself—in the sentence "I wouldn't mind going round to make love with Annette", for example—instead of a normal expression like "have it off" or "get my rocks off".

"Make love", that's the sort of sissy talk I never thought I'd hear myself say. Which just goes to show: never say never. Ever.

Or just catching her unawares, seeing her at any time, the hair at her temples damp with sweat, the way she has of biting her lip when she feels pleasure, the little cries she makes, all that stuff. Thinking about her even when we're doing it and still thinking how beautiful she is. The weirdest thing was when I stopped getting out of bed straight after we fucked. When I started lying there, all calm, her head on my shoulder, not even wanting to get out or to chuck her out of bed. That was the point where I knew I was in a bad way. I decided it was best to be careful. Not make it too obvious that I felt good being with her. Not leave my weak point exposed, if you get what I mean.

Landremont often says:

"A man can't fall any further than when he falls in love."

Me, I say it's just verbal diarrhoea.

For one thing, Landremont was madly in love with his wife. And for another thing, like I told you before, the guy's an arsehole.

I MADE MISTAKES with Margueritte too, at the beginning. I didn't want to let her know straight off that I found her funny, that I was learning things from her. I didn't want to seem too familiar either, which was just as well because she kept her guard up, too. She was friendly, you know? But polite.

Usually I'm suspicious of people like that. People like Jacques Devallée or Berthaulon, the new mayor, who talk in a way so complicated they drown the baby in the bathwater of smart arsery. When guys like that make fun of you, they do it so politely that you end up thanking them.

Me, I wasn't "well brought up". I was knocked into shape with sticks and stones like a stray dog in the street. (That's a figure of speech. My mother was crazy, but she wasn't that crazy.) Let's just say my childhood was no picnic.

The upshot is that I'm not exactly tactful sometimes, and I know some people find me a bit rude. When I try to express myself, I can tell I shock people from the way they twist their mouths a little or the way they wrinkle their noses like something stinks.

The problem is that I have to explain what I think using the words I've learned. And that makes things difficult. That's probably why I sometimes seem too direct, because I'm always talking in a straight line. But a cat is a cat and a twat is a twat. It's not my fault these words exist. I don't make them up, I just use them. It's not worth flogging a dead cat over.

At the same time, I have hang-ups about it. Not so much because out of every fifteen words I say, ten of them are swear words, but because fifteen words usually isn't enough to say what I want to say.

Landremont says that power will always belong to orators. And he makes a big deal of it, pounding his fist on the table, all smug, because he obviously thinks he's one of them.

"To *orators*, Germain! Do you understand? To or-a-tors!"

He can lord it over me all he likes, no one's going to die and make him king of the world.

He talks better than me, I'll give him that. But what use is that if he's got nothing to say?

All this to get back to the fact that even though Margueritte seemed completely harmless, with her little smiles and her sentences, I thought that sooner or later she'd end up treating me like a pathetic moron. But she always talked to me like I was a person.

And you see, that can change a man.

W HEN SHE TALKS about herself, Margueritte looks so happy you wouldn't believe it. She's so hungry to tell me about her life, it must taste like jam.

My life tastes like a shit sandwich but someone forgot the bread.

She's been all around the world and back again. The deserts, the savannahs and everywhere in between. When you look at her in her flowery dress, her stick-thin legs and her goody-goody expression, you'd think she was a nun or a nurse or maybe a teacher. But no, she used to head off and camp out with tribes of headhunters, she slept under mosquito nets. It makes me laugh, thinking about it. I look at her and I think, This little granny is really someone.

She tells me about these amazing adventures, she says everything that happens can teach us a lesson, serve as an example, help us to stand taller. When it comes to standing tall, I don't need any help: I was at the front of the queue when they were dishing it out. But I think I'm starting to get the idea that what happens can teach us a lesson. If everything was piss easy, what would we do with all the happiness? Happiness needs to feel like a lucky break, either that or you have to earn it, but it needs to be rare or expensive, otherwise I don't see the point. That's not very well put, but I know what I mean and that's the main thing. Being happy is all about comparisons.

And on top of everything, for lots of people in the world, happiness is in danger of extinction just like the Jivaro Indians, or gorillas, or the ozone layer. Not everyone gets served a big dollop of happiness. If we did, I think we'd know.

There's nothing communist about luck.

O NE DAY, I talked to Margueritte about all these questions that have been going round and round in my head lately—since I met her, I'm pretty sure, though I didn't tell her that.

I told her I couldn't stop them, they repeated on me like a dose of garlic, these whys and wherefores that were doing my head in.

Margueritte smiled.

I said, Why are you smiling?

"Because you're asking yourself all these questions… It is the defining trait of man."

I didn't dare tell her that the defining trait of man mostly applies to women, because, when it comes to questions, they're capable of churning out a sackload at least ten times a day.

Besides, I didn't want to annoy her, so I just said:

"I wouldn't mind… if I had any answers!"

"Oh, you will not always be able to find answers… It is posing the question that matters, don't you think, Germain?"

Oh dear, I thought, if my opinion matters then we're really in deep shit.

But at the same time—and this is what's surprising—it's impossible not to answer Margueritte's questions. You should see her, the way she waits patiently, her hands resting in her lap, her back straight. Her way of saying: Don't you agree,

Germain? (or a different name if it's you she's talking to) and you feel you have to come up with something. Anything, so long as you can think of something, and fast. Because if you didn't say anything, you'd feel like a bastard. Like Santa Claus showing up empty handed on Christmas Eve.

So I said:

"Well, the thing is, I don't really see what good it does to spend your whole time asking questions and never knowing the answers, not that I'm trying to boast."

"And yet I'm sure it is something you have often experienced…"

"What?"

"Come, come… Surely there must be times when you feel you don't completely understand? During a conversation, for example?"

And I thought, Bingo! She's finally realized I'm a brainless moron. And that knocked the stuffing out of me.

She went on:

"I know that whenever it happens to me, it makes me want to search for a solution. I suffer from spadework syndrome."

"From what?" I said, though it was only about the last word, because I know all about spadework.

She laughed.

"Spadework syndrome: when I come up against a problem, I try to thin things out."

I know a lot about thinning out too—I thin out my turnips.

Margueritte went on:

"That's simply the way it is: I have a need to understand. It's the same with words. I adore dictionaries!"

"Me too," I said.

I only said it to make her happy. I mean, I'm not a barbarian. Only it was a barefaced lie, because if there's one book that makes me queasy it's a dictionary.

She opened her eyes wide and said:

"You too?"

I was glad to have made her happy by getting the answer right.

"Yes, yes…" I said, trying not to sound like I was bragging in case she asked me trick questions to see if I'd read it right through to the end.

But she just nodded.

Afterwards, we talked about this and that and finally came to pigeons and animals in general. One thing led to another and in the end I rummaged in my pocket and took out a cat I had whittled from an apple branch Marco gave me.

Margueritte said:

"Oooooh…"

And then:

"It's so beautiful! It really is striking. So delicate, so natural…"

I said, "No, no, it's nothing."

She said, "Oh, but it is, Germain, it is lovely."

So I said:

"Go on then, you have it. It's a present."

"I couldn't possibly accept," she said, holding up her hand, "It must have taken you hours…"

I said:

"Did it heck, I knocked it up in nothing flat."

Which wasn't true, seeing as how I'd worked my arse off for two days solid to make that cat. Particularly on the ears and the paws.

I only said it so she wouldn't feel awkward, and it worked, because after that she didn't make any objections.

Sometimes, if you let people know you're attached to something, it stops them from accepting it. It's not what you give, it's how you give, as my mother used to say, and she never gave anyone anything.

I DON'T REALLY KNOW why I do it. Whittle pieces of wood, I mean. It started when I got my first penknife at about twelve or thirteen. I'd seen it in a display case at the tobacconist's. A beautiful Opinel No. 8, stainless steel blade, beechwood handle. Thinking back, I thought about it all the time.

It's weird, there are things that become as important to you as actual people. I had that experience with a teddy bear when I was a kid. Patoche, his name was. He was ugly as sin, one eye had been sewn back on and most of his fur had come off. But he was *my* teddy. I wouldn't have been able to sleep without him, I would have felt like a brother-less orphan.

Sometimes I think that maybe it's the same for Annette. That I'm her teddy and she doesn't see me with her eyes, she sees me with her heart.

Anyway, all I could think about was this Opinel, with the rounded handle and the rotating safety catch. I knew straight off what I could use it for. If I had it, I'd be able to take it fishing, for example. A knife can be very useful when you're fishing. You can use it to cut back reeds, to look less of an idiot when you're eating, to fight off snakes. And while you're at it, you could use it to gut trout. But no matter how many times I counted the money in my piggybank, I knew I'd never have enough to buy it. But as the Good Lord said (or maybe it was one of His apostles): *God helps those who help themselves!*

So one morning I swiped it from the case when I went in to buy my mother's cigarettes. I helped myself. Why should it always be other people and not me?

Those display cases have locks a two-year-old could pick. If I was a shopkeeper I wouldn't trust them.

I had it for nearly ten years, that knife. I stupidly lost it one morning, in fact when I was going fishing. I would have been better off staying home. They say: be sure your sins will find you while you're out. And, incidentally, if that's true, there are people out there who should be really worried.

Actually, I think the reason I like whittling is because it keeps my hands busy.

I'VE BEEN THINKING about the word *uncultivated—land that has not been tilled; see also: fallow ground*—which popped into my head one day while I was talking to Margueritte. And about how the cultivation in books relates to the cultivation of artichokes. Just because land isn't cultivated doesn't mean it's not good for potatoes and other things. Make no mistake: tilling doesn't make the soil better, it just prepares it to better accommodate the seedlings. It aerates it. Because if the soil is too acidic, too chalky or too poor, nothing will take root.

I know what you're going to say. You're going to say: What about fertilizer?

Let me tell you something about fertilizer: you can dump a truckload on the land, but if the soil was bad to begin with, it'll still be bad. OK, maybe with a lot of sweat, you might get three or four potatoes out of it. Spuds the size of marbles. Whereas if you have rich, black soil with thick clods that don't crumble between your fingers, then with or without fertilizer, it will produce something. Then you have to factor in the know-how of whoever's doing the gardening. And the weather, which depends on the Good Lord, who makes it rain whenever it suits Him. And the phases of the moon, because you'd have to be a complete idiot to plant during the young moon if you want roots—carrots, beetroot, onions—or during the old moon if it's leaves—lettuce, spinach, cabbage—but I'm not telling you anything you don't already know. Then there's the tricks you never tell anyone, except on your deathbed, such as the best places to find mushrooms—even just saying that, I crossed my fingers. May the Good Lord keep me hale and hearty and equal to the task.

All this leads me to the conclusion that with people, it's just the same: just because you're uncultivated doesn't mean you're not cultivable. You just need to stumble on the right gardener. Find the wrong one, one with no experience, and you're a botched job.

And I'm not just saying that about that bastard Monsieur Bayle who obviously didn't know how to sow by the moon, if I can be metaphorical—*see also: symbolic.*

Anyway, these are just a couple of ideas that popped into my head without me noticing.

Daydreaming helps me think.

A FEW DAYS AFTER our conversation about questions and answers and dictionaries, I got to the bench to find Margueritte was already sitting there and next to her was a package in fancy wrapping paper.

I pretended not to notice and sat down the same as always.

She nodded to the package and said:

"It's for you."

"For me?" I said.

It wasn't my birthday. Not that I wasn't happy: it's always nice to get a present when you're not expecting something. Even when you are expecting it, I suppose. Though I don't have much experience of that.

Margueritte gave a little shake of her head. She said:

"Actually, strictly speaking it's not a gift, it is something I have owned for a long time, something that has served me often…"

"But why?" I said.

"Why what?"

"Why would you give me a present?"

She gave me her surprised look.

"Don't you think it's possible to give someone something for no reason, just to make them happy? Why, only last week you spontaneously gave me that adorable kitten carved from apple wood…"

Margueritte has a different way of thinking from other people. From the people I know, at least. I can't imagine Landremont or Marco handing me something and saying:

"Here, Germain, I just wanted to make you happy."

That said, I can't imagine giving them a little sculpted cat. Spontaneously or otherwise.

We're not queers.

My mother didn't really go in for giving presents. But seeing as how I got a present of a clip round the ear every day, I didn't expect much on my birthdays. I thought about everyone I knew, but Annette is the only other person who could have done something like this, for no other reason than because she loves me.

Since I was just sitting there, saying nothing, Margueritte asked:

"Don't you want to know what it is?"

I said: Yeah, of course!

Feeling it with my fingers, I worked out it was a book. Shit. I unwrapped it anyway, doing my best to look interested, because you don't judge a gift horse by its cover. It was worse than a book: it was a dictionary.

Oh shit! I thought. What the hell am I going to do with this?

I said thank you to Margueritte. But, in all honesty, it was a bit of an effort.

And she, looking like someone who's just pulled off some brilliant April Fool's trick, said:

"Well, I'm relieved to see that you like it! I was worried I might be making a mistake, giving it to you."

"Nuh-uh," I said, "It's a brilliant idea… Actually, I was just about to buy a new one…"

She said:

"Really? Is yours past its sell-by date?"

And she gave a little laugh.

I like it when she laughs. But at the same time it scares me, I'm always afraid she won't be able to catch her breath. You see old people who start laughing and end up coughing and spluttering like a diesel engine, something goes down the wrong way and before you know it they've croaked.

Though it's as good a way as any to die.

"Germain, do you know the *true* purpose of dictionaries?"

I felt like saying: For propping up a wonky table, but instead I said:

"For understanding difficult words."

"Well, that too… But not just that. Above all, they allow you to sail away."

"?…"

"Let's imagine you are looking up a word, all right? Some word that you find 'difficult'."

That wasn't very hard to imagine.

"Very well. You find the word and next to it you sometimes see the letters *s.a.* followed by one or more other words. It stands for *see also*, but it could just as easily stand for *sail away*. It urges us to turn the pages, to track down new nouns, adjectives or verbs which in turn send us off again in search of other words…"

Suddenly, she was all excited. Old people get their kicks very differently from the rest of us, I swear.

So, anyway, I said, Yeah, obviously, of course, and I'm staring down at my feet.

"A dictionary is not simply a book, Germain. It is much more than that. It is a maze… an extraordinary labyrinth in which we joyfully lose ourselves."

I don't know much about labyrinths, unless you count the maze they create around the bridle paths at the Château de la Mort for midsummer festival, next to the ghost train and the rollercoaster, but if that was what she was talking about, I didn't see the connection to this dictionary of hers, and certainly not to having fun.

So, I said, Uh-huh, but I didn't add anything, I just nodded.

She kind of carried on raving for a bit, then she calmed down and we were able to talk about other stuff, mostly about her research into seeds, which are like tiny boxes "comprised of an integument that protects the albumen and an embryo".

I know what an embryo is, it's got something to do with hens' eggs and with babies, too, and that suddenly makes me think of Annette. One of these days I'm going to give her one, there's no getting out of it.

Albumen, on the other hand, doesn't mean anything to me.

I explained to Margueritte that from grape seeds you can make grape seed oil. And she said, Yes, you're absolutely right! And that they contain other ingredients including tannin, a word I know really well seeing as how you get it in wine.

It's funny, you think you're talking about scientific stuff but no, it turns out you're on home ground.

WHEN MARGUERITTE got up to leave, I walked her as far as the bandstand and then turned and headed straight home without popping into Chez Francine. I couldn't see myself showing up for a drink lugging a dictionary with me. In my crowd, books aren't exactly welcome. A little bit is all right, but you can't go overboard. When it's Landremont, people accept it because he's the oldest and the only mechanic. Even Julien, who passed his *baccalauréat*, or Marco who speaks five languages—Italian on account of his origins, Serbian and Romanian on account of his illegitimate stepfathers, and Spanish for the past ten years—even they don't go around showing off how clever they are. So it wouldn't look good, what with me being soft in the head—*see also: foolish, half-witted*.

I went straight home without making any detours, I was scared of running into someone. I was so ashamed I stashed the dictionary out of sight like it was a porn mag. And that's what was weird, because I felt the same overpowering urge to look inside. It just goes to show.

That night, I hesitated. And then I thought, why don't I look up a difficult word just to get an idea? *Labyrinth*, for example.

And that's when I realized there was a catch: to look up a word in the dictionary, *you have to know how to spell it*! Which means dictionaries are only useful to educated people, who are precisely the ones who don't need them.

People are hacking down Amazon rainforests with chain-saws to make dictionaries that are supposed to help you but only end up proving how thickheaded you actually are? So much for the ecosystem!

It's not Margueritte's fault: she was born on the right side of the book cover, reading and writing comes naturally to her. Since I didn't want to waste her present, I decided to look up a few things I felt pretty sure I could spell.

Fuck and *shit*, yes. *Slut*, too. *Imbecile*, no.

Olympique de Marseille, nothing doing, but *Saint-Etienne*, result!

I have to say, it's pretty comprehensive for an old dictionary.

After that I looked up people's names just for a laugh. I didn't find Landremont, or Marco, or Zekouc-Pelletier, Youssef, Francine or Chazes.

I found Margueritte, with only one *t*, which is a type of daisy. And Annette, with no *e* and a *th* which means dill, so I looked up dill which turns out to be a herb you can eat raw, something I'd happily do with my own Annette.

I found two entries for Germain, but with different spellings.

Germane: *(adj.) relevant to a subject under consideration*

German(e): *(adj., archaic) a sibling sharing both parents, as opposed to a half-sibling or step-sibling, from Latin* germanus *"genuine, of the same parents"; s.a. cousin-german, German*

Since there was an *s.a.* for *see also* before *cousin-german*, I went to have a look but I didn't really understand the explanation, so in the end I looked up German: *(n.) a native or inhabitant of Germany, or a person of German descent.* Germans: *the tribes of Germania (Burgundians, Franks, Goths, Lombards, Saxons, Suevi, Teutons, Vandals)* and I filed it all away in my head just in case.

I've got a really good memory when it comes to memorizing.

Next, I looked up *sparrow*, which is *a passerine bird with brown plumage streaked with black; may refer to birds of similar livery.*

Livery, on the off-chance that you don't know, means *clothing or uniform bearing the colours of a king's coat of arms* which has got no connection to sparrows, but by extension it can also mean *the distinctive coat or plumage of an animal or bird*, which obviously is connected.

I have to say I was a bit disappointed by the entry for *tomato*, where it says: *annual herbaceous plant (genus: Solanum; family: Solanaceae) widely cultivated for its fruit*, which is fine, as far as it goes. But further on it says, *see also: plum tomato.* Well, I'm sorry, but no. Because *Solanaceae*, fine, no problem, but why only plum tomato? Why make people think that's the only cultivar? Are dictionary writers paid to keep things short or what? Do they keep the entries brief to save on paper, or is it because cultivated people don't know shit about things that are actually cultivated?

It's not like I was trying to find fault with Margueritte's present, but in this case I knew a hell of a lot more than her dictionary, seeing as how, from personal experience—off the top of my head, without even looking them up—I can reel off loads of tomato cultivars: the Tonnelet, the Saint Pierre, the White Beauty, the Black Krim and the Santorini, the Orange Bourgoin, the Black Prince, the Goutte d'Eau, the Roma, and the Gioia della Mensa, not to mention the Marmande and the Picardy.

"YOU KNOW, trying to find anything in that dictionary of yours is like a blind man in a dark room looking for a black hat that isn't even there."

Margueritte raised an eyebrow.

"A blind man…"

"It's a figure of speech, it means it's complicated."

"Oh, I see… But in what way is it 'complicated'?"

I'd been fretting about this all night and all the way there that morning.

I had to let it out.

I thought, fuck it, just say it, so I gave it to her with both barrels, about how I hated reading, about not being able to spell, about that bastard Monsieur Bayle, the whole farrago.

Now we'll see, I thought.

But Margueritte just gave me a funny look.

I was still laying it on thick, all the stuff I'd never been able to get out that was still stuck in my throat. How you get treated like a halfwit—me especially—if you don't know how to read properly. How people think that education is a substitute for politeness. How they talk down to you the minute they realize you've only got a handful of words while they speak like they've swallowed an encyclopaedia. But scratch the surface of what they're saying and it's mostly bullshit and hot air. I went on and on, by now I was practically shouting.

Even though I could hear it in my head, that little voice yelling: *For God's sake, shut up, Germain! Can't you see you're freaking out this poor old woman?* But I couldn't shut up, it just poured out of me, the whole haystack of straws that broke the camel's back, the injustice, the whole shebang. And the worst thing was that just listening to myself made me even more scared. It was like putting my life into words was like spilling salt on the wound. Inside I was a mess, and these pictures were flashing past and my inner voice was begging the Lord in His great mercy to gag me so I'd shut my trap. And then all the rest of it came out: the girlfriends, the job, the dreams I had as a kid. And to cap it all, my mother.

Lastly I told her that her dictionary wasn't even complete, because *Solanaceae*, fine, no problem, but plum tomato!…

Anyway.

Margueritte took a long deep breath; it was like I'd been holding her head under water.

And she said:

"Germain, I'm so sorry."

That took the pressure off straight away.

"Why are you sorry?" I said.

"Listening to you, I realized that you are right: if one does not know how a word is spelled, or the way it works alphabetically, a dictionary is utterly useless!"

"And no offence, but it's not even comprehensive."

"Ah yes, that is another point I cannot dispute. Not two days ago, I looked up the word *klingon*—and would you believe it, it wasn't there!"

"I'm not surprised. And I can tell you right now it's not the only word missing!"

"Probably not, probably not... At the same time, you have to admit that there are many things you *can* learn from a dictionary..."

"Fair enough, but if I can't even use it..."

"Very true... Tsk tsk. It is frustrating. What are we going to do?"

She sat there thinking, her hands and her head shaking a little. I was racking my brain to think of something to help, because she'd said *we*, and that made me happy.

In the end, I said:

"I mean, if you just knew how to write the word you're looking for, then you could just go to the right page..."

"Exactly."

"Like, if I wanted to look up, I don't know... let's say *labyrinth*, though why I came up with that example, God knows..."

"And God works in mysterious ways. Oh, the French language is a difficult thing. For example, the word *labyrinth* is littered with traps. Here, let me show you." And then she delved in her handbag, took out a pen and went back to rummaging again.

"You wouldn't have a notepad on you?"

"Uh... no."

"Perhaps a scrap of paper?"

"I've got my shopping list, if that's any good."

"That will be fine, Germain, that will be fine."

She wrote down the word, tilting her head, leaning on her handbag. Her handwriting was large and slightly shaky, but not too shabby for her age. She held out the piece of paper.

"There you go."

La-by-rin-th?

Bloody hell. I'd never have guessed that.

A FEW DAYS LATER, walking along the avenue du Général de Gaulle, I noticed that someone had tagged the new multimedia library—there was graffiti all across the front. Obviously, we all talked about it down at Chez Francine. Marco laughed, shrugged his shoulders and said it was no big deal since it was just some kid's tag and not Nazi swastikas and stuff like that. And it would give the lazy bastards on the municipal street-cleaning crew something to do, because they never did a tap of work. Francine didn't say anything, seeing as how she was still really broken up about Youssef. Landremont was angry. He kept saying the little shits responsible should be tarred and feathered, that would make an example of them. Julien nodded his head and said:

"Honestly, it's a real shame. I mean, it's pretty crap, the new library building, but at least it was clean. And it's our taxes that'll pay for it, you mark my words, because they're not going to restore the place for free. And they'll have to repaint the whole front of the building, so it's not going to come cheap, let me tell you!"

"They tagged the other side too, on the rue Faïence," I said.

"Jesus wept," Landremont roared, "The evil little shits. Vandals, that's what they are, vandals!"

"Yeah," I said, "Vandals, that's what they are. And Saxons. I blame the Saxons."

They all looked at each other, confused, and Julien said:

"What the hell has this got to do with saxophones?"

"*Saxons*, I said Sax-ons you know, like Teutons, or Lombards."

Landremont shook his head and said:

"Sorry, I've no idea what he's on about. You guys?"

The others shook their heads.

"Explain it to us, Germain, because right now we're completely stumped."

"What do you want me to explain? Do you know how to speak the language or don't you?"

If there's one thing you don't wind Landremont up about, it's culture and vocabulary. He always knows the answers to the quiz show questions on TV, he's got a head full of information that's as useful as a chocolate teapot, like *Name a fruit of the Solanaceae family* (tomato).

I knew I'd touched a nerve from the way he combed his hand across his bald head, like he was expecting to find his hair. In the end, he said:

"Could you be a little more specific as to what you're talking about?"

"You're the one who brought up the subject. You mentioned the Vandals, so I added the Saxons and the Teutons. I just thought of them at random, I could just as easily have said… I don't know… the Burgundians."

"Is he drunk or what?" said Julien.

"No, I'm not drunk. You should get out more: I was giving you examples of the Germanic peoples."

"Really?" said Marco, "Were there any swastikas?"

"Bloody hell, it's like you're doing it deliberately. I said 'Germanic' from 'Germania', I wasn't talking about the Nazis."

"Not all Germans are Nazis!" Landremont said angrily.

Then, straight after, he turned to me and said:

"What made you bring that up?"

"What made me bring what up?"

"All those names, Burgundians, Lombards…"

"Saxophones…" said Marco.

"Sax-ons," said Julien.

I yelled:

"But like I just said, *you're* the one who brought it up first. You were the one who said that taggers are Vandals, that's why I—"

Landremont banged his fist on the table.

"OK, guys, I think I get it."

"Bully for you," said Marco.

Landremont jerked his chin:

"Can you give us a list then, of these Germanic peoples?"

"No problem! There's Burgundians, Franks, Goths, Lombards, Saxons, Suevi, Teutons, Vandals…"

Landremont sniggered and repeated:

"…and Vandals… There you go. And in alphabetical order, no less!"

Marco groaned.

"If this is some private joke, just say so. We'll leave you to it, you can turn the lights out when you go."

Landremont gave me a wink.

"Way to go, Germain! You never cease to amaze me. The other day you were talking about Camus's *The Plague* and today it's the ancient tribes of Germania… What's next? Are you going to start quoting Maupassant to us?"

"Stop it," said Julien, "Just give him a break!"

But when he smells blood, Landremont is like a dog with a bone, he locks his jaws shut and there's nothing you can do. So, just like that, he said pointedly:

"Because obviously you know about Maupassant, right?"

"Yeah… Of course, yeah."

"So tell me, what sort of things did he write?"

"Fuck off," I said.

"Oh come on, just for a laugh."

"Fine, then! He wrote that guidebook, *Le Guide Maupassant*, OK? I'm not a complete fucking moron."

Julien coughed into his glass. Landremont raised his eyebrows.

I finished my beer. Then I got up and left without another word.

And then, just as I was going out the door, I heard Landremont yelling: "*Le Guide Maupassant!* Jesus H. Christ! Did you hear that? *Le Guy de Maupassant!*"

"Yeah, so what's your point?… I've never heard of it," said Marco.

"Is it like *Le Guide Michelin?*" said Francine.

I was too far away to hear any more. But I didn't care, because I'd made Landremont look like a knucklehead. For once.

For a while now my mother's been going round the bend. But recently it's more of a hairpin. These days, I see her shuffling down the garden at all hours, looking like she's been dragged through a hedge backwards. She'll stop in front of the runner beans, or the potatoes—it varies—and she'll stand there like a statue, looking like she's thinking, then traipse back up the path with her empty basket.

Whenever I go to see her, it's like a fireworks display. I'm lucky if she even opens the door.

She's got it into her head that I'm after her pension. She's told all the neighbours that me and my friend are planning to kill her. She follows me around the house screaming that she's not about to let herself be ripped off, and how I'm a disgrace, torturing my mother like this.

Anyway, she's won; I've thrown in the towel, I've given up.

I'm not going to set foot in her house, I'm not going to bring her vegetables to make soup or fix her taps or change the light bulbs or anything. I say this to myself, but I go anyway, and I hate myself for being such an idiot.

She calls me a bastard. If I get too close, she tries to wallop me. Some days, it's all I can do to stop myself giving her a good slap. Just to shut her up.

When I've finally had it up to the back teeth, I talk to the guys at Chez Francine, I spill my guts.

Julien gives me the usual spiel. No matter what you do, Germain, she'll always be your mother. In this life, we only get one mother.

Just as well we don't get more than one, I think, otherwise you might as well give me two planks, a hammer and some nails and I'll make my own bloody cross right now.

Landremont says it's understandable for me to feel angry because anyone would have to admit that my mother is like a dose of salts.

More like a dose of rat poison.

The other day, Marco asked me why I don't put her into assisted living.

"Dump my mother in an old folks' home? She's only sixty-three. You think it would be easy, explaining that to her? I'm not about to risk it, I can tell you."

Landremont explained that I could get someone to do it for me.

"And I suppose you could personally drag her there? You with your scrawny little arms?"

"Hang on a minute, she can't be that bad!"

"You've obviously never seen her when she's foaming at the mouth."

Julien said:

"He's right, when his mother's angry, she puts the fear of God in me."

"She could put the fear of God in God," I said. "So to get her out of the house and into a care home, I don't see how it could be done without sending in a SWAT team…"

Francine protested that we were going a bit too far.

"I mean it, I don't know what it is with men, they always have to exaggerate… Your mother isn't that bad, Germain. She's a bit gone in the head, that's all."

"She's like a fish," Marco laughed, "rotting from the head down."

I reminded him that this was my mother he was talking about.

Marco said, OK, fine, no need to get riled, and then to calm things down he told us about his grandfather, who claims that microphones have been planted all over the house, especially in the toilet.

"Microphones?" we all said. "Who would want to bug your grandfather?"

"He says it's the town hall, that they're spying on him."

"On the toilet?"

"Yep."

"Shit!" we said.

And then Jojo said, You have to admit, there's no upside to being old.

THESE DAYS I work at SOPRAF Painting and Restoration.

I got the job through Julien's brother-in-law, Etienne. I do the heavy lifting. Unpacking the tins of paint, stacking the shelves, taking the boxes and the plastic to the recycling, that sort of shit, it takes in a whole range of things I know how to do.

Jack of all trades, that's my area of expertise.

Down at the Manpower office, they know me. They know my talents don't come with degrees and diplomas. But when it comes to hauling sacks of cement on my shoulder while chatting and joking, I'm a genius. Whenever they have a thankless task—*see also: difficult, unpleasant*—that no one wants to do, they give it to yours truly, sorted.

Some people work in offices with wall-to-wall carpets and plastic plants, and other people—like me—sweat blood for three euros an hour.

That's life, what can you do? We've all got our own shit to deal with.

The problem with jobs is that you have to have one in order to live. Well, you have to hold one down for long enough to be eligible for unemployment benefit afterwards. Otherwise, I have to say work doesn't much interest me. Well, not when it's hard graft.

Landremont says my problem is that I have no ambition.

I say Landremont's problem is that he has too many opinions.

I think a person can be normal and not like work. Actually, it's the opposite I find surprising. You have to remember that there are billions of people all over the world who manage to live without having jobs. The Jivaro Indians, for example. When I was a little kid, my dream of the future didn't involve lugging breeze blocks or unloading palettes or humping truck tyres. And it didn't involve a career on the dole. Apart from the powerful vocation I already told you about—rose window-maker—I wanted to be an Amazonian Indian. My uncle Georges had given me a book about them with loads of photos he'd found in a bargain bin.

For a long time I kept it in the bottom of the wardrobe in my bedroom.

On days when people were making my life hell (Monsieur Bayle, or Cyril Gontier—my greatest enemy back then—not to mention my mother, who always got the gold medal), I'd take out the book in the evening, snuggle up in bed and look at the photos.

I pictured myself as an Indian chief in a brand new feather headdress, my dick swinging in the breeze in its penis sheath. And I'd think to myself, If they don't stop making my life a misery, I'll whittle some poison darts and shoot them in the arse. Then I'll stand there with my blowpipe, all casual, and watch them die slowly and painfully as they froth at the mouth.

You've got big dreams when you're a kid.

All the same, being an Amazonian Indian seems pretty cool to me.

They wander around pretty much naked apart from a necklace and a bow and arrow, they do sod all apart from playing the pan pipes and having little wars every now and then. They sit around campfires getting plastered on booze made from jungle creepers and I don't know what all, they smoke spliffs for religious reasons.

They've got it good. And they get to see naked women all day long without even making an effort, since their women go round with their tits out and their other bits hidden by a feather. They fish, they hunt, they collect plants—to make poison for the darts. They grow a few gourds, some manioc, a bit of tobacco. They don't spend their whole lives lugging crates. If you want my opinion, their lives are heaven on earth.

The only problem is that, when Landremont is banging on at me about my future and saying:

"For God's sake, Germain, you can't carry on like this for the rest of your life. You're forty-five years old, surely there's something you want to be when you grow up?"

I can't say:

"I want to be a Jivaro Indian."

First off, he'd think I was mad as well as being soft in the head. And secondly, knowing him, he'd start lecturing me about the hole in the ozone layer, and oil and multinationals

and deforestation, about Blackwater fever and malaria—
which are God-awful diseases—and end up with a national
disaster where every living human being in Amazonia dies.

I don't know whether it's because his wife died or because
he got cirrhosis, but lately Landremont's turned into the
kind of guy who can turn heaven into a shit tip in a couple
of sentences.

He crushes all hope, he pours weedkiller on it.

T O BEGIN WITH, I found Margueritte funny. And educational too, from the conversation point of view. Then, little by little, I got attached to her without even realizing.

Affection is something that grows on the quiet, it takes root without you knowing, then overruns the place worse than Japanese knotweed. By then, it's too late: you can't dose your heart with Roundup to weed out feelings.

In the early days, I was just happy to see her sitting on the bench when I arrived.

Later, if she wasn't there, I wondered what she could possibly be doing instead of coming to see me.

Later still, after we'd discussed cultural things and stuff, I thought back over our conversations.

Sometimes, when she was reading, I'd stumble on a word I didn't know—*prestige, exorbitant, languorous*—and I'd give her a little sign and she would explain it for me, or she'd write it on a little notepad she'd bought especially, because that had become the way we did things, and at night, when I got home, I'd look up the words.

Exorbitant—*see also: expensive, outrageous, prohibitive.*

She even made little reminders for me. She had written out the alphabet in order in big letters on a sheet of white paper. And for every letter, she'd also written the letters that came second and even third.

Ab, Ac, Ad…

Aba, Abc, Abd…

She must have spent ages doing it, but it was really useful, seeing as how it's not enough to know where *R* is, if you're looking up *reminisce*: you need to know that it comes before *repartee* and after *rejuvenate*.

I pinned it up beside my bed, and every night before I went to sleep I'd read the alphabet, out loud: A, B, C, D… And then I'd think of examples from everyday life. A is for Annette, B is for ballsack, C is for carrot, D is for dipstick, etc. Margueritte was with me even when she wasn't around.

And then, one particular day when she wasn't in the park—I mean we don't meet up every day, obviously—it hit me: I didn't know a thing about her apart from the name that she was christened with. Even if I was being tortured, I couldn't have given her surname to the cops.

I realized that if something serious happened, a stroke or something, no one would come and tell me because I didn't have any entitlement—*see also: rights, prerogative*—so I'd never know, she'd be off dying somewhere and I'd never see her again. I tell you, I was shit-scared, like some little kid lost in a big department store. I tried to reason with myself. Get over yourself, Germain, she's just some random old lady. But no matter how much I tried not to care, I spent the whole day worrying and fretting. And so next time, as soon as I clapped eyes on her, I asked her her address straight out, point blank.

"I've been living in a retirement home called Les Peupliers for the past two years. It's a stone's throw from the town hall, just opposite the square, do you know the place?"

I said: Uh-huh, sure I know it.

Too right I knew it, I'd worked as a labourer there four or five years ago when they were renovating the upstairs rooms. In fact, let me tell you they'll be bloody lucky if a chunk of ceiling doesn't fall into some old codger's morning coffee one of these days, because they didn't understand the concept of a load-bearing wall at that retirement home. I mean, it's solid enough, if you don't look too closely. If we get hit by an earthquake some day, I can't answer for the death toll. Though obviously I didn't tell Margueritte that. It was just something I thought to myself.

Margueritte went on:

"It's a lovely home, I'm glad I chose it: the staff are always available, and they're so caring."

With the money they charge, they can hardly afford to be uncaring.

"And what's your surname?" I asked out of the blue.

"Escoffier, Margueritte Escoffier, why?"

I could hardly say: In case some day I have to come and dig you out of the rubble. So I said:

"No reason. I just wanted to know."

And *bang*! she was off at a gallop about "the desire to know, that insatiable curiosity peculiar to mankind", and so fourth and fifth and sixth. I let her ramble on, she loves a good discussion. And it doesn't cost me anything to sit there and pretend to listen. You can still be human. After that she talked about her life at Les Peupliers: Scrabble, bingo, trips to museums, the kind of shit that could make you want to top yourself.

It was like Margueritte was reading my mind, because she sighed and said:

"No one wants to grow old, you know…"

Then she gave a little laugh and added:

"But the great benefit of being old is that when you're bored, you know it won't be for long."

I said: You're not wrong there.

She went on:

"I can't complain: I've still got my health, I live in pleas-ant surroundings. My pension is more than adequate. No, honestly, it would be unseemly to feel sorry for myself. But growing old… Growing old is a nuisance."

This made me think about my own situation and realize that, if I take after my mother, me getting old would be a nightmare for everyone concerned and one I'd be better off avoiding. All because of the bloody genetic traits you can't help inheriting on account of genealogy. Not to mention all the defects I don't know about because they're from the bastard side of my father and his lot.

By the time I'd stopped thinking, I realized that Margueritte had stopped talking.

We don't often look at each other, her and me. That's normal with a park bench, because you're sitting next to each other. Usually, we chat away and watch the kids with their pedal cars playing at being Michael Schumacher. Or at the clouds, or the pigeons. The important thing is that we listen to each other, we don't need to look. But seeing as how she wasn't saying anything, I gave her a once-over. She looked really down in the dumps. I can't stand seeing a kid or an old person looking sad. It makes me sad too. And before I could stop myself, I'd put an arm around Margueritte's shoulders and kissed her on the cheek.

She gripped my hand—she looked like she was about to shed a little tear—and she said:

"You are a good man, Germain. Your friends are very fortunate."

What are you supposed to say to that? If you say yes, you come across as an arrogant wanker.

If you say no, you sound like a two-faced bastard.

I said, "Well…"

That seemed to be all right.

Margueritte gave a little cough, she said:

"Now then, if I'm not mistaken, we said we would do a little more reading together, did we not?"

"We did."

"But we have not done any reading since *Promise at Dawn* several weeks ago, have we?"

"Um… no."

"We shall have to remedy the situation! What would you like me to read next time?"

"Well… um…"

"Is there a subject that particularly interests you?"

"…"

"History, for example? Adventure stories? Detective novels? I don't know, perhaps—"

"Amazonian Indians!" I butted in.

And as soon as I said it, I figured it was going to make me seem like a prize idiot.

But Margueritte said:

"Ah, the Amazonian Indians, of course… Of course… In that case, without wishing to get carried away, I think I have a novel on my shelves that you will enjoy…"

I wasn't even surprised: when you've got books about plagues, you're bound to have something on the Jivaro Indians.

"Is it by Camus?" I asked.

"Oh, no, not this time. But it is very good nonetheless, you'll see."

I said OK, and that was the truth.

T HIS IS HOW Margueritte came to read me *The Old Man Who Read Love Stories*. She showed up one Monday looking very pleased with herself. She took a little book out of her bag and patted it and said:

"This is the book I mentioned to you the other day."

"About the Amazonian Indians?" I said.

"Yes, among other things," she said.

"It's pretty short," I said.

She told me you don't judge a book by its length.

"Any more than you can judge a person by their height," I said. "As long as both feet touch the ground, you're tall enough, isn't that right?"

And straight away I felt terrible and I looked down at her stumpy little legs dangling in the air. When it comes to park benches, she's not grown-up size.

She saw where I was looking, shrugged her shoulders and laughed. She said:

"Shall we begin?"

"Go for it!" I said.

So she began:

"*The sky was a donkey's swollen paunch hanging threateningly low overhead.*"

"That's a metaphor," I said.

Indeed it is, she said, and that made me happy.

And then she went back to reading and everything else followed.

I have to tell you: I never knew I could love a story so much.

I had liked *The Plague* because it had reminded me of that incident—*see also: event, episode*—where my neighbour had his head eaten by his dog, and whatever happens people always cling to childhood memories. And besides, I was fascinated by the idea of the teeming rats and all that stuff. The other book, the one by the guy whose mother loved him too much and vice is versa and who's always looking for springs and wells and never finding them because life doesn't keep its promises wasn't bad either, and that one was pretty long.

But *The Old Man Who Read*... wow! I couldn't get enough, even when a cute girl in a tracksuit jogged right past with her breasts bobbing.

I was hanging on every word like a tick hanging on to a dog.

First off, I liked it because it was short. Then it killed two birds with one stone because it taught me a whole bunch of stuff about the Jivaro Indians, also known as the Shuar, though it means the same thing. For example, they file their teeth into points and they never get toothache, which is just as well for them because jungle dentists are vicious thugs! You only have to read the start of the book, when all the poor guys from the village come to be butchered by some bastard dentist called Dr Loachamín—who curses and swears as he rips out their teeth and replaces them with second-hand dentures that don't even fit, to go by what Margueritte read:

"Now then, how about this set?"

"It's too tight. I can't close my mouth."

"Hell, what a delicate bunch we are! Come on, then, try another one."

"It's too loose. It'll fall out if I sneeze."

"Well, don't catch a cold, you fool. Open your mouth."

I could see them as clearly as if I was there. It was even more lifelike than Albert Camus. I felt my feet tingling because it reminded me of when I was a kid, going to our dentist, Dr Tercelin, who used to give me a clout if I moved because he was hurting me.

"Sometimes a patient let out a scream that frightened the birds, and knocked the forceps away in reaching with a free hand for the handle of his machete."

I would have laid into him with the machete, I can tell you. Dr Tercelin was a real bastard, he used to scream at us kids if we came on our own, but when our mothers came with us he was all lollipops and barley sugar. My mother used to dump me there and go off shopping on the pretext that the smell of ether made her stomach heave-ho. When the torture was finished, I would go and wait for her on the front step, with a gum abscess and a nasty taste of cloves in my mouth. I tell you, I could have done with finding a fucking well!...

I'm remembering all this stuff while I'm listening to Margueritte, and I'm thinking, It's crazy how a book can dredge up all this stuff from the past.

Margueritte read me the whole thing, she didn't skimp:

"Take it like a man, you ninny. I know it hurts, and I told you whose fault that is. Don't take it out on me. Sit still and show you've got spunk."

Just hearing her say the word spunk was worth it.

On the other hand, when I wanted her to reread a passage I didn't dare ask her. So I pinned back my ears and tried to remember everything.

The Jivaro people are no fools, let me tell you. They blacken the blades of their machetes before they go hunting so that monkeys won't see them glinting in the sunlight. I should do that with my Opinel. They've got snakes ten metres long and as thick as my thigh and huge catfish that weigh sixty-two kilos. I'm not likely to catch anything that big down at the lake any time soon.

But I can just imagine myself, proud as a Jivaro, showing up at Chez Francine with a seventy-kilo catfish. Marco would have a fit, him being champion regional fly-fishing poacher and all.

He's a good guy, Marco. Just don't go wounding his pride.

I also learned that Amazonia is a shit heap of a place. It's always bucketing down, it's full of nothing but mud and scorpions, nothing like I imagined it, and that's a real disillusion—*see also: disenchantment, disappointment.* The other disillusion is that Shuar couples never kiss each other on the lips. No pecks, no tongues, nothing.

On the other hand, when they make love—I prefer to say "make love" these days—the woman squats down over the man, because she finds that *this is the ideal position for feeling the love*, which I have to say would suit me fine, without wanting to spill the details of my personal private life.

Anyway, this book I'm talking about is the kind of thing I'll read again and again in my life if the Good Lord spares me from cataracts and Alzheimer's, but it's His call, it's not up to me to tell Him what to do.

When all's said and done, now that I know more about the situation—thanks to Monsieur Sepúlveda—I can see that the Jivaro plan is not a good one. The book my uncle gave me didn't have all these details, but it was in a bargain bin, and that's probably why.

Margueritte gave me this book when we had finished reading, which took about a week. And she said:

"Germain, I may not be able to read to you for very much longer, I'm afraid…"

"Why, are you fed up?"

"No, of course not! It has been a real pleasure. It's just that I don't see clearly any more…"

"Is it cataracts?" (Because I'd been worrying about getting cataracts myself.)

"No, unfortunately," she said, "It's rather more serious."

"Glaucoma?" I said, because my mother's got that and a bunch of other things I'll probably inherit.

"No, not that either. It's something incurable. They call it age-related macular degeneration. It's a rather pretentious name for an illness, don't you think?"

"I don't know, but it sounds complicated. What's it like?"

"A blot in the middle of the eye which is already making it difficult for me to read. Very soon, everything directly in front of me will be grey. I will only be able to see at the sides."

"Shit!" I said.

Then I added, Sorry.

"Oh, please, don't apologize. I think in certain cases it is perfectly permissible to use the word 'shit'."

"But can you still see me? Now?"

"Yes, of course. But in a little while, I will not be able to recognize you. I will not be able to see faces, to read, to sew, or to count the pigeons."

It felt weird, her telling me this. Especially as she didn't make a big deal of it, she just quietly explained it.

I thought to myself, As shitty diseases go, it's a shitty disease, and may the Good Lord forgive me, since He's the one to blame for it.

Margueritte said:

"What I will miss most of all is reading."

"Me too," I said.

And you see, that's something I thought I'd never think. Let alone say.

I WENT HOME with this thing burrowing into my brain faster than a drill into a lump of balsa wood. Margueritte losing her sight. All the books she wouldn't be able to read. That she wouldn't be able to read to me. I heard that voice inside me that's always making comments when I'm frustrated. For once at least it wasn't yelling. It was broken, like me, and saying: *Germain, do whatever you have to, but you can't leave the old dear like that.*

"Oh really? And what am I supposed to do? Give her a squirt of Windolene and hope it demists her eyes? What the hell can I do if she's going blind?"

Shut up, Germain. For once in your life try thinking before you speak.

I was thinking: She's not even going to be able to play the Lotto or Scrabble any more, and she'll miss that although, personally, I don't see the point of them.

I went round and round in circles like a cat when you hide its litter tray. I was thinking, Margueritte is not as strong as she makes out. She's knee-high to a chickpea, she's old as Methuselah. A soft breeze and she'd go down with flu. Oh, she puts on a brave face all right. She laughs and she laughs, but what is she going to do all alone, surrounded by grey, without even her books for company? It's bad enough that she never had kids. I was beating myself up about it, it was like a slap in the face, and that's when I knew—it was a bit confused, a bit rough around the edges—I couldn't let Margueritte down. Whatever I did now, it was too late, she already had me with that little laugh, the flowery dress, the blue rinse. Eighty-six years old, and all that to wind up with a white stick? What the bloody hell is the Good Lord up to these days? I thought. I don't care if He's pissed off, if He can't take criticism, He shouldn't go around creating things.

I said to myself, Margueritte is going to lose her sight and *I'm* going to lose Margueritte and our little talks on the park bench and all the My dear Germain, did you know?…

When she can't see any more, she won't be able to come and I'll have lost everything: the little cheat sheets so I don't take a wrong turn looking things up in the dictionary. The books. Everything.

I realized that no matter what I did, I couldn't change the fate of Margueritte's destiny. The bloody disease, macular matriculation or whatever it was, would keep going until it had done its job and Margueritte was blind.

And that thought made me as sad as a lump of lead.

When you love someone, that one person being unhappy can cause you more pain than all the people you hate put together if they tried to screw up your whole life.

One day, Margueritte quoted some African writer, a Monsieur Bâ, who said something that's really simple but really smart: *When an old man dies, it is a library burning*, or something like that. Well, that's exactly how I saw the problem now. I felt like best mates with this Monsieur Bâ, even though the two of us have never actually met. Except in this case, just my luck, the library being torched was mine. And the worst thing was it was burning down just when I finally found it on the map.

And you have to understand that that was unbearable, even for a metaphor.

Seems like I'd spent my whole life looking for a spring or a well. So if the Almighty was planning to cut off the water supply now, I would howl like a dog too. Because I had to face facts: Margueritte mattered to me. She was like a grandmother, only better, because the only grannies I know are the non-existent one on my father's side, or the one who shows up once in a while and screams at my mother.

I think that's when it came to me. The idea of adopting Margueritte. I know you're not legally allowed to adopt a grown-up senior citizen. But it's a bad law, I think you should be able to. If everything had turned out the way it should have, I'll tell you what would have happened: Margueritte would have had a daughter. Later on, that daughter would turn out to be my mother—not my actual mother, someone different and a lot better—because I would have been the love child of her and my father instead of being born by mistake. We'd all have lived happily ever after like idiots. The end.

But why would the Good Lord make things simple when He can make them complicated? I'm not criticizing Him or anything, but I'm pretty fucking angry.

I thought to myself, Margueritte talks to me, she even listens to me. If I ask her questions, she answers them. She's always teaching me things. When I'm with her, I never think about the gaping hole inside my head waiting to be filled, I just think about all the stuff I already owe her.

So people can make fun of me until the end of all eternity and treat me like a bonehead, I didn't care any more: Margueritte was my fairy grandmother. With a wave of her wand, she'd turned me into a flourishing garden. I had been a patch of fallow ground, but now, because of her, I can feel things growing, here are flowers and fruits and leaves and branches, as Landremont says when he's trying to pick up girls, though I've never really understood why he says it.

Margueritte was my fountain of knowledge. And because of a twist of fate, maybe soon I would be the one complaining that *there are no more springs, only mirages*, to quote poor Romain Gary.

I was pretty bloody hacked off with God and this time I wasn't about to apologize.

I don't really care that He doesn't grant my wishes, that He makes my life shit. I've never been a brown-noser, saying my prayers and genuflecting and all that stuff. I know the whole Our Father who art in heaven thing, and a few other bits and pieces, Thy kingdom come, Thy will be done, Amen, and off you trot. I never set foot in church except for weddings and christenings and funerals.

I suppose I'm living in sin, if you take the Ten Commandments literally.

The third commandment, for example, I've definitely taken His name *in vain*, and the fact that I was drunk isn't really an excuse.

With the fifth, *Honour thy father and thy mother*, He's the one who did a bad job.

Thy father, I never had. *Thy mother*, I've had it up to here.

When it comes to *Thou shalt not commit adultery*, I haven't really *really* sinned, it's just that He's set the bar a bit high, because if you listen to Him, he says *whosoever looks at a woman with lust for her has already committed adultery with her in his heart.* So that rules me out, because I'm sorry but one look at Julien's wife or Jacques Devallée's, and I've got a hard-on.

When it comes to number eight, *Thou shalt not steal*, I'm not exactly squeaky clean either, what with my penknife and a bunch of other things I'm not going to list—this isn't a tax return.

With all that, if the Almighty doesn't want to have anything to do with me, it's my own fault.

But Margueritte?

She's kind, she never bothers anyone, she reads like someone on the radio, but she's the one who gets it in the neck? It's wrongful injustice! I know loads of people who spend their lives being vicious and spewing bile who'll wind up, at ninety-five, fit as fiddles, dying peacefully in their own beds. It makes you think that bile pickles bastards the way vinegar pickles onions.

I was so disgusted, I ended up talking about the whole situation to Annette.

It wasn't easy, because when you're revealing things you never know where it's going to end.

You think you're just going to mention a couple of things, but it's like when someone waxes the top step, you take one step too far and *bam*! you find yourself at the bottom of the stairs, bruised and battered at having revealed so much.

Talking about Margueritte felt very indiscreet of me. I never thought there would be so much explaining to do. Because, obviously, I had to tell Annette where the two of us first met, and talk about the park where I spent most afternoons farting around, because being on my own in the caravan makes me panicky—and I can hardly spend all day working on the vegetable garden, especially when my mother keeps turning up like a scarecrow. And I had to tell her about the hours I'd spent listening to this old granny reading me stories. About the conversations we have about life, about pigeons and Klingons and all that. About the books she gives me that I read with my highlighter marker, running my finger under the words because otherwise I get completely lost: I end up reading the same line three times and not under-standing a bloody word. Not to mention the dictionary that I use all the time now, thanks to the cheat sheets Margueritte makes for me—how will I manage when she's not around? And I talk about the fear of never being able to read anything by myself because if Margueritte doesn't read me the whole book, I'm scared the words will go in one eye and out the other without stopping for me to understand.

I didn't tell Annette everything. It was bad enough having to tell her I was a pathetic prick with the reading age of a not very bright seven-year-old. So I didn't go into the whole thing about the war memorial, the pigeons. We'd burn that bridge later, I thought. Maybe.

Annette had tears in her eyes when I told her about the disease with the complicated name I couldn't remember.

She said:

"The poor thing, what can we do to help?"

I said: There's nothing we can do, that's what's pissing me off.

She said: I understand.

"I don't think so," I said, "I don't think you really under-stand, about the books and all that stuff."

"It doesn't matter, you know, I don't care if you're not very good at reading. You're good at other things. And I can read books to you."

"Have you got any?"

"Not many. But we can get some from the library on the rue Émile Zola."

"Yeah, but have you any idea how much books cost?"

"They don't cost anything, it's free to use the library. My sister takes her kids there and they're allowed to borrow three books for two weeks."

I said: Are you allowed to borrow less than three?

She said: You can borrow one, or none if you don't feel like it, it's no problem.

"And can you keep it for longer?"

"I don't really know. I think eventually you have to pay a fine. I'll ask my sister."

After that we talked about other things for a bit, and then we stopped talking, except with our hands.

She's got a hold on me, that woman, it's like she smears herself with glue: the minute we touch, I'm stuck on her. It's like two magnets.

Magnet to magnet, opposites attract.

I CALLED ROUND to see Youss'.

It came to me on the spur of the moment, off the cuff. I showed up at about eight p.m., it's the best time to catch him at home.

He opened the door. I said:

"Have you lost your mind or what?"

He said:

"Hey, want some tea? Come on in."

I sat on a pouffe just to be civil and all, though I really hate them—I never know where to put my legs and I end up with cramp.

Youssef said:

"You seem a bit wound up."

I didn't beat around the bush.

"What the hell is going on with you and Stéphanie? Is it true you're together?"

"Yeah. Mint tea or ordinary?"

And at this point I realized I was evolving as a species, because instead of giving him practical advice, you know, like: Good for you, she's really hot. Go for it! I said:

"So what about Francine?"

Youssef shrugged.

"I don't really know, you know? I'm in two minds."

"Have you got feelings for her, for Stéphanie?"

"I don't really know. I think I just got carried away, she was always hanging around, and she's crazy hot…"

I couldn't exactly prove the opposite. She's got a pair of tits on her, I swear, one look and you're hard enough to drill through concrete.

"She's a bit young, though…"

"Yeah, and Francine's not young any more, that's the problem. But I still feel good when I'm with her. That's what's bugging me. I don't know who to pick."

He seemed in a real state. I'm kind of like a father to Youssef, I talk to him like he was my son.

"Aren't you worried about getting your cock caught between two stools with all this dicking around?" I said.

"What would you do if you were me?"

"Wha?… well, um… I'm not you. It's bad enough being me, so excuse me but—"

"How is she coping, Francine?"

"How do you expect? She spends all day crying."

"Shit."

"Exactly. Listen, do you mind if I sit on a stool, 'cause this big bloody cushion wrecks my knees."

"Come into the kitchen. I've made *chorba*, you want some?"

We talked about Francine, about Annette, about our mothers—particularly about his, who died when he was nine. Not everyone can be so lucky.

Youssef told me that what bugs him most about Francine is that she's past her sell-by date when it comes to giving him kids. And Youss' is crazy about kids, he brought up his five sisters. Especially Fatia, the youngest, who's seventeen now and mad as a fish in a raincoat but she's stunning and she's got the whole world wrapped around her finger, the little Klingon.

So Youss' can't imagine life without bottles and nappies, something I would have thought was completely twisted in a guy not long ago. But the strange thing was that, just listening to him, I kind of understood where he was coming from.

"Are you sure Francine can't give you a baby?"

"I don't know, she's forty-six, so…"

"Well, why don't you adopt, then? Maybe she can't make kids, but she'd know how to bring one up. Miserable kids aren't exactly thin on the ground, you know."

"You think so?" he said.

"I don't think so, I know so."

"Yeah, but there's sixteen years between us…"

"So much the better: with the time difference, you'll both croak round about the same time rather than her ending up a widow, which is what usually happens. Honestly, you're worrying about nothing."

"Maybe you're right," he said.

We left it at that, and as I walked home I realized all we'd talked about was women. And that I was missing Annette, and not just her body either.

So I went round to her place.

I'VE THOUGHT ABOUT IT.

And I've come to the conclusion that if Annette can read books to me, the least I can do is try to read a couple by myself. All the way through. If I can do it, then maybe I can read to Margueritte when she's not able to see any more.

This is what I thought.

I went to the library, because Annette mentioned it, and because of Monsieur Bâ talking about old people dying. It's really good, it's free admission.

Inside, there were books, truckloads of them. It was enough to put you off reading because, like Landremont says, too much choice is no choice at all.

I stood there like a lemon, not knowing how to make up my mind, and after a few minutes the woman behind the desk said:

"Are you looking for something in particular?"

And I said:

"A book."

"You've come to the right place. If I can be of any help…"

"That would be good, thanks," I said.

"Do you know the title? The author?"

Pff, what the hell did I know?

She seemed to be waiting for me to say something.

I thought, If I carry on like this, she's going to figure out that someone like me has no business being here and throw me out. So I said:

"Actually, I don't want *a* book... I want a book to read, that's all."

She said:

"All right, good, I understand..."

And she gave me the kind of smile you get from sales reps:

"Documentary, essays, fiction?"

"No, nothing like that, a book that tells a story, you know?"

"So, fiction, then. Any particular kind?"

"Short," I said.

"Perhaps an anthology?"

"No, nothing about science. A made-up story."

"You mean a novel?"

"Yeah, a novel would be all right. As long as it's short."

She got up and went over to the shelves, muttering to herself:

"A short novel... a short novel..."

"An easy-to-read one, if you've got it."

She stopped and said, Ah? Then she said:

"For a child of what age?"

She was starting to seriously wind me up.

"It's for my grandmother," I said.

At that point some guy came in with two kids and waved to her.

The lady walked off and said to me, I'll be right back, have a look, the adult section is over there.

She pointed to six bookcases measuring about three metres by one metre eighty high in polished beechwood veneer with chamfered uprights and dovetailed joints. I wandered between them for a while, taking out a book here, a book there.

But there were too many of them, and they all looked the same, or nearly the same, and that put me off. And then I saw a little boy over in the children's section. He was looking at the titles and frowning, he would pick out a book, read what was on the back cover and then put it back. A bit farther along, he would take out another book, and start all over again.

I thought to myself, Hey, that's not a bad idea, I'll read what they say about the story and that might help me choose.

It didn't help at all.

I have to say, when you look at what they put on the back of novels, it makes you wonder if they really want you to read them. It's not aimed at me, I can tell you that. A whole string of convoluted words: *inexorable, fecund, exemplary concision, polyphony...*—not a single book where they just write: this is an adventure story or a love story—or a book about Indians. Zilch.

I was thinking: If you can't even understand the summary, how are you going to understand the book, you fathead.

Me and books were off to a bad start.

That's when the woman came back and asked me:

"Did you manage to find what you were looking for?"

I didn't know how to say no, so I showed her a little book I'd just picked out at random and said, Yes, it's fine, I'll take this one.

She looked surprised. I felt miserable. But I thought, oh well, once a moron always a moron.

"Do you think my grandmother will like it?"

She smiled.

"Oh, yes! Absolutely. I'm just surprised because you said you weren't looking for short stories but… no, it's a very good choice. It's a beautiful book, particularly the fable that gives the anthology its name. Poetic, deeply moving… I'm sure she will love it."

Then she filled out a form for me and said:

"You can keep books for two weeks, and borrow up to three books at a time."

I said yes, thank you and goodbye.

As I left, I looked at the title: *Child of the High Seas.*

I wondered what it would be about.

I DIDN'T OPEN IT straight away. I waited a couple of days. Sometimes, I'd pick it up and look at it. I'd open the cover a crack, like a dirty old man looking up some girl's skirt, then quickly close it and head off to Chez Francine, or to work in my garden.

And then I heard my inner voice saying: *What are you pissing about for, Germain? Scared of a little book? Have you even thought about Margueritte?*

Then I thought, Right, I'll give it a go, but if I don't understand *all* the words—or most of them—on the first page, I'll give it up as a bad job.

So I started reading.

How did it come to be built, this floating street?

So far, so good. It didn't mean anything, but at least I understood the words.

What sailors, with the help of what architects, had built it in the high Atlantic on the surface of the ocean, above a chasm six thousand metres deep? Six thousand metres, take away three zeros, that makes sixty—no, that makes six kilometres.

A chasm six kilometres deep? Shit, that's really deep! Six kilometres.

Wow.

This winding street… these slate roofs… I still had no trouble understanding.

…these humble immutable shops?

Ah, shit! I thought, Here we go! Im-mu-ta-ble. Right…
A, B, C, D…G, H, I.
Ic, Id, Il, Im, got it.
Im-a, Im-b, Im-i, Im-m…
Imma, Imme, Immi, Immo, Immu… OK.

Immutable—*that which forever remains the same, that which cannot be changed.* So, shops that don't change. Like Moredon, on the rue Paille who's so tight-fisted he probably hasn't repainted the front of his bakery in twenty years, and he really should because it's starting to look scuzzy.

I carried on to the bottom of page one, which ended:
How did it remain standing, without being tossed about by the waves?

There.

I had read the whole page without too much trouble, and I don't want to blow my own trombone but I'd managed to understand every word except one.

I didn't really know where the story was headed, but I turned the page.

And on the next page there was a little girl, twelve years old, walking alone on this liquid street—which I had a bit of trouble imagining at first, but in the end I figured it probably looked like the ones in Venice. A little girl who fell asleep whenever boats appeared on the ocean. And when she fell asleep, the village disappeared beneath the swell—*see also: wave, breaker, roller*—with her.

And no one knew that this little girl existed. No one.

There was always food in the cupboards and fresh bread in the bakery. Whenever she opened a jar of jam, *it remained utterly intact.* She should have patented this thing, because that would have been really interesting to community associations, especially for school dinners and meals on wheels for senior citizens.

She spent her time looking through old photo albums. She pretended to go to school. Morning and evening, she would open and close the windows. *At night, she lit candles, or she sewed by the light of a lamp.* And me—and I know this is dumb—but I felt sad, thinking of her, the poor kid, lost in the middle of nowhere. Never in my whole life—not even in a book—had I met anyone so alone, so completely at sea.

I got to the end pretty quickly, it only took me three days—because it's not just one story, this anthology thing, it's a lot of short stories one after the other.

I read the last section again, the one that starts *Sailors who dream upon the high seas…* to make sure I'd understood. Then I started at the beginning again. And again.

I could see her sitting alone in a classroom pretending to listen to a teacher. And then doing her homework like a good girl. I thought, I bet she sticks out her tongue a bit when she writes, and she gets ink on her fingers, she probably crosses things out—I made loads of mistakes when I was her age.

But she was a whole lot neater than me, the copybooks were perfect.

She would look at herself in the mirror, and she was slow to grow up.

And I could really understand that, because when you're a kid, the only thing you really want is for it to start. Life. You only do stupid things to kill time.

You spend years dreaming of being a grown-up, only to end up missing what it was like to be a kid.

Anyway, that's just an aside—which means an incidental remark not intended to be heard by everyone.

When the *little freighter belching steam* came through the village, I thought the little girl was going to be saved. But no. And when a wave comes looking for her, *a colossal wave*, with *two eyes perfectly simulated in foam*, to try and help her die, and it doesn't work, it completely freaks you out, let me tell you—at least it did me.

But the weirdest thing about the story is that, the more I read it, the older this kid got inside my head. The more she seemed like Margueritte, actually. She became an old shrivelled little girl, tiny as a sparrow, with the eyes of Margueritte and her blue-rinse hairdo.

And the more like Margueritte she seemed, the more choked up I got when I reread the end, when it talks about a creature *that cannot live, nor die, nor love, and yet suffers as though it were living, loving and constantly on the point of dying, a creature utterly dispossessed amid the watery wastes.*

I couldn't tell you why, but I felt that somewhere inside Margueritte was that sad little girl, waiting for the wave that never came.

The things you imagine sometimes.

B EFORE, I NEVER looked at Margueritte in detail. I'd see her in the distance, coming along the path, inching towards me. Or she would be sitting on the park bench, waiting for me. We'd say hello, count the pigeons, do our reading, but we didn't sit staring at each other like china dogs. These days, I observe her.

Observing means looking carefully at something you want to remember. And when you observe, you see better. Obviously. You even see things you'd rather not have noticed, but that's just tough luck.

For example, when she writes—and when she reads, too—she turns her head slightly. At first, I thought it was funny, this new habit. I thought, Hey, she's like a bird, with that little tilt of her head, looking at everything sideways. But that's not it. She turns her head so she can read, because she already has trouble seeing what's in front of her. Margueritte can only see life out of the corner of her eye.

And when she walks, you can see her hesitate. At least if you observe her, you notice it.

These days, when we go our separate ways, I always walk her all the way to the gate on the boulevard de la Libération. I'd be ashamed to let her go by herself.

I say, I'll go with you, Margueritte, I'll walk you to the gate.

She says, Oh, no, Germain, that's very kind, but there's no need, I wouldn't want to take you out of your way.

I tell her it's no problem. And it's not exactly far, it's about 200 metres. But to old people, metres probably seem longer.

"And besides, I don't want to waste your precious time…"

I've got time enough to burn. What would I save if I stopped wasting it?

I walk next to her. You might almost say *above* her, given how tiny she is—I've got at least fifty centimetres on her.

Sometimes I have an urge to take her arm, when I see her detouring instead of sticking to the middle of the path. But I let her get on with it, as long as she can stand on her own two feet. I wouldn't want to humiliate her. So, when she goes too far off course, I go round to the other side of her—no one's any the wiser—and I gently steer her towards the middle.

When we leave the park, I wouldn't dare follow her back to the old folks' home. I stand there by the gate and watch her walk away, tottering like an old duck.

I keep an eye out, just in case.

I think about her having to deal with all that traffic, the pedestrian crossings, the people jostling her, all that shit. I feel like following her, forcing the cars to stop, scaring off the people so she has the footpath all to herself.

And I realize that caring about a grandmother isn't any easier than falling in love.

It's the opposite.

I PUT IN as much time as I needed to be able to read properly. But I'm stubborn like that.

Then one afternoon, when Margueritte sat down next to me on the bench, I said:

"I've got a surprise for you!"

She said, "Oh? Really?"

And then she said: I love surprises.

"You're all woman, aren't you?" I said.

She laughed and she said: Oh, let's just say more of a relic...

She explained the word and I laughed too.

"So, tell me then, this surprise?"

"Close your eyes," I said.

She probably thought I was going to give her a present—chocolates or I don't know what.

I just said, You'll see, it's poetic and moving.

And I started and—you probably won't believe this—I was scared half to death.

"How did it come to be built, this floating street?

"What sailors, with the help of what architects, had built it in the high Atlantic on the surface of the ocean, above a chasm six thousand metres deep?

"That's six kilometres," I explained.

She smiled without opening her eyes.

So I carried on.

I admit I'd been practising. First, just in my head, then

later out loud. And then in front of Annette who would say, Wait, yes, that's good, a little slower, a little louder—it almost sounded like we were making love.

"*The child believed she was the only little girl in the world. Did she even know that she was a little girl?...*"

Margueritte sat, listening quietly, her hands in her lap. And it felt strange reading out loud in the middle of a park for fourteen pigeons and one little old lady.

And at the same time as I was carrying on with the story, I was thinking—on a different channel—If that bastard Monsieur Bayle could see me now! Him and all the rest of them! Everyone!

I think I was proud of myself.

I stopped on page thirteen, just after *The child of the high seas had no sense of what a far-off country might be, nor Charles, nor Steenvoorde*—I mangled that last name, *Ste-en-vo-orde*, but I don't speak foreign and there's no subtitles to give you the pronunciation.

"Would you like me to read the rest to you some other time?" I said, "Because right now I have to take it back to the library. But I'll borrow it again if you want. I don't mind, it doesn't cost anything."

Margueritte opened her eyes and said:

"Germain, that was such a lovely surprise. I don't know how to thank you."

And then, just afterwards, she said:

"Although... I have an idea. Would you like to come back with me to my apartment one of these days?"

"Sure, of course. I can come right now if you like."

"I'm not putting you out?"

"It's no problem."

That day, she didn't read to me, because I'd already done the business. She just asked me to read the rest to her some other day, if I would be so kind.

I said, Yeah, sure, if you'd like me to.

I would have been pissed off if she hadn't wanted me to, given how much time I'd spent learning to read it aloud, this bloody story that was so poetic. Oh, and deeply moving.

Afterwards we talked about this and that and nothing in particular.

At some point she said unexpectedly and completely out of the blue:

"I'm afraid I shall have to get myself a stick before long. I'm finding it difficult to see obstacles and hindrances now."

"Does that make you sad?"

"Well, to be candid, let us say I'm finding it difficult to adjust to the prospect…"

"What kind are you planning to get, wood or metal?"

"Oh, I'd much prefer wood. Metal makes it seem like a prosthesis. I'll come round to the idea when I'm an old lady… I've got a little time before then, don't you think?"

I laughed. She laughed too.

I said:

"The reason I asked is because I know where you can get really nice walking sticks in carved chestnut. It's this guy I know, his family have been doing it for generations. Would you like me to take you there? We could go on Sunday? It's less than an hour by car, it's all back roads and I don't drive fast."

"You'll think I'm being ridiculous, Germain, but I get terribly carsick unless I'm the one driving… Back when I used to drive, it was not a problem but, alas, getting behind the wheel now is out of the question. I'd be a public menace."

"I can go myself, I can take my girlfriend. I'll bring back a catalogue."

"Well, if it's not too much trouble… I have to admit, I would feel proud to walk through the park with a beautiful chestnut cane…"

"OK, that's what we'll do then."

She asked if I still wanted to come back with her.

I said yes, of course. I'm not the kind to blow hot and cold.

She lives in an apartment the size of a postage stamp. Bedroom-living room-balcony. But it's well situated, not too noisy, not too stuffy. It's fine. It doesn't have a garden, but it's fine.

She showed me beautiful things she'd brought back from all over the world. Then she said:

"It's your turn to close your eyes now, Germain… And no peeking, promise?"

"I promise."

I heard her open a drawer and rummage for something. Then she came over and told me to hold out my hand.

She put something in my hand, something heavyish and a little cold.

"You can open your eyes now."

I opened them and said, Shit! and then quickly, Oops, sorry!

"It's really beautiful, I can't accept it…"

"Please, for my sake."

It was a Laguiole pocket knife, top of the range—it was stunning. Damascus blade in forged steel, horn-tip handle, brass bolster and plates, and a beautiful leather sheath for carrying it.

The sort of knife that costs a bomb and a leg, even for a Jivaro Indian.

"I have to give you a coin in trade," I said, fumbling in my pocket.

"A coin? But why?"

"Because otherwise we'll fall out. Didn't you know that?"

"No, no… explain it to me."

"When you give someone a knife, he has to give you some shrapnel—some small change in trade. I've only got twenty centimes on me, but it's not the amount that matters. Put it to one side, don't spend it."

Margueritte held out her hand, very serious.

She said, Oh, oh, in that case I must find a secret place to hide this precious treasure…

One of the reasons I like Margueritte is because she's a bit bonkers.

I DID AS I PROMISED. I went to see them, the chestnut walking sticks. But on my own. Not that I was trying to get away from Annette, but I had an idea rattling around in my head and when that happens it's best not to crowd me. I know Baralin, the guy who makes them.

I said to him, Clément, I want a nice one, sanded but not varnished.

"Is it for you?" he asked.

"No," I said, "It's for my grandmother."

"What size is she?"

I said, Well she comes up to about here on me...

"OK, let's go for the children's size then. She doesn't sound very tall."

He got me to pick from a pile. I took two, in case my hand slipped.

For a while, I wondered what I was going to carve and whether I was just going to whittle the handle or the whole length of the shaft. I've never whittled anything for anyone, except when I was a kid, a little sheep for Hélène Morin, because I was in love with her, only she made fun of me, showing it to everyone in school, the bitch. I put a jinx on her every day for at least a month.

Later on, she married that fat bastard Boiraut. I figure that makes us quits.

But this was completely different.

I decided on the head of a pigeon, with the neck stretched out the way they do when they're looking for crumbs, it was perfect for the curve of the handle. And the beak I carved as a relief, so it would be soft against the palm of the hand and rounded at the end. With a soldering iron, I burned two holes for the eyes, and they made it look so lifelike you wouldn't believe it. Then I sanded it with P120 fine-grade emery paper, buffed it with a chamois and, finally, I varnished it. It took a hell of a time, but God damn it was stunning!

When I'd finished, I stood it opposite my bed.

Annette told me it was magnificent, and she even slept over that night.

I got up twice during the night pretending I needed to piss, but that was just an excuse so I could look at the walking stick. I haven't got prostate trouble yet.

I T WAS TIME for me to give my present.

When I saw Margueritte at the far end of the path, I felt my heart hammer.

I got up, I held out the walking stick, I said to her, It's for you.

There was nothing else I could have said.

She looked up at me, head tilted to one side, but only just. She took the walking stick, she gently ran her fingers over the handle again and again. It was like she was stroking a real pigeon.

I asked her:

"Do you like it?"

"Oh, I have to admit, it's not unattractive…"

Not unattractive? I was hurt like a stab in the back.

"That is litotes, of course," she said.

"No, it's a pigeon," I said.

She smiled.

"Litotes is a figure of speech, Germain, a way of emphasizing a point, using a negative to affirm a positive. It is saying black the better to say white. For example: 'it's not unattractive' actually means that I think it is extraordinarily beautiful. A real work of art. And I am very touched."

And then she added, suddenly sounding very shaken:

"Because you did it, didn't you Germain… you carved the cane?"

"With the knife you gave me." I said.

This wasn't true: I can only really carve with my Opinel and a wood chisel. But I didn't see why telling a little white lie about it would bother the Almighty, after all the ninth commandment just says *Thou shalt not bear false witness against thy neighbour*. God doesn't say you can't lie in other cases. And who am I to be more Catholic than the Pope?

In any case, Margueritte was very touched when I mentioned her knife, I could tell, she gave a little tearful *oooh* and she squeezed my hand. All afternoon, I didn't see her put down that cane. So you see I was right to lay it on with a trowel.

After a little while, she said:

"Germain, did you know that there are four-hand pieces written for piano?"

"There are what?"

"Some pieces of music are written for two people to play together on the same instrument. Well, only on the piano, actually…"

"Well it would be pretty tough to do on a tin whistle."

She gave that little bell-like laugh of hers and said:

"So, I was thinking, I mean only if you agree of course… I was thinking that we might read together, while there is still time?"

"A four-eyed story, you mean?"

And then I said: Of course.

I'll enjoy that.

T HE NEXT DAY, a bunch of us were down at Chez Francine, holding the fort while she was out shopping. I took out my new knife to clean my nails, all casual.

Marco said:

"You lucky bastard! That's a magnificent beast!"

"Any chance of a look?" said Julien.

Landremont studied it from every angle, opened and closed it and ran his thumb across the blade like he knew a thing or two about knives.

"A fine piece of craftsmanship," he said, "Where did you get it?"

"It was a present."

From who? they asked.

I said, vaguely:

"From my grandmother."

"*Your* grandmother?" said Landremont, "You mean the one we know, your mother's mother?"

"My grandmother," I repeated.

"That old bat? She's taken to giving you presents these days? I thought she hated you and your mother…"

"You have to admit the women in your family are all psychos," said Marco, "You're lucky you haven't got a sister."

I was about to tell him to get off my back when Jojo came in and sat down next to us.

He said:

"Wow, that's a hell of a beautiful knife you've got there."

And before I had a chance to say anything, he added:

"Listen, guys, we're going to have to say our goodbyes soon. I'm moving, I've found a job in Bordeaux."

We said, Oh?

Julien pointed out that it's not exactly next door.

"But it is a beautiful city," said Landremont, who hardly sets foot outside his garage, but he reads a lot of magazines.

Marco said:

"What about Francine? Have you told her?"

"No, I was planning on leaving tonight without a word…"

"That's not very nice…" said Marco.

"Yeah, and more importantly, it's not true. Of course I've told Francine! What do you take me for, you moron? You think I'd do a moonlight flit? I've given my notice, and I'll stick around a bit longer if necessary to train my replacement."

Marco shrugged.

"Honestly, I'm not sure this is a good time… Francine will wind up going off the rails. It was bad enough Youssef dumping her without you leaving too…"

Jojo laughed and said:

"Oh, I wouldn't worry too much about that. Francine's feeling a lot better since last night…"

We didn't ask him why because right at that moment she came in with a big smile on her face and Youss' trailing behind her carrying the shopping bags.

"Oh, I see… So you've made up, then…" said Marco.

Youssef gave us a wink and said, Give me a minute to sort things out in the kitchen and I'll be right back.

"Your sex life is your own business!" said Julien with a laugh.

We joked for a bit while we waited for Youssef, and when he showed up Landremont said:

"Looks like Francine doesn't hate you as much…"

Youssef said: What do you mean "as much"? She doesn't hate me at all, why would she hate me when I came back to her? Has she said something?

Landremont roared:

"Oh, stop flapping like a headless chicken, it was just a joke."

And I said:

"It was an example of litotes."

"An example of what?" Youssef said.

"Litotes. A way of saying black the better to say white, if you like. She doesn't hate you as much means: she loves you. God, you can be slow on the uptake sometimes."

Landremont sighed.

"Litotes. That's it exactly."

But he was looking at me nervously, the way he does these days whenever I say something intellectual. For a minute I almost thought he was going to put a hand on my forehead to see if I was running a fever.

He said:

"Don't take this the wrong way, Germain, but I hardly

recognize you. I'm not sure I didn't like you better before, because these days you scare me."

Marco said:

"It's true, you've changed. You hardly drink any more, you don't tell dumb jokes, you come out with words no one understands. If you're not careful, pretty soon Annette will be the only girl you're screwing…"

I didn't say anything.

It's true that I used to make them laugh. I'd tell dirty jokes, or jokes about Belgians and Jews and blacks. No Italian jokes, on account of Marco, or Arab jokes, because of Youssef. Friends are off limits.

Nowadays I've realized that those jokes aren't really funny. But when you're drunk, the bar is lower, you'll laugh at anything. And it becomes a habit, you know, being an ignoramus. I can say that from experience.

It starts out because you're lazy, but then the wind changes and you're stuck that way.

Then one day, counting pigeons, by complete coincidence you meet a grandmother who's surplus to requirements and you end up with *The Plague*, the Jivaro Indians and poor Monsieur Gary who's still crying for his mother. And that little girl in Venice, except it's really the middle of the ocean. Not to mention the dictionary, which is actually an absorbing book given how you get completely sucked in when you try to find a word. And gradually, you see everything differently. You're interested in different things. You stop fucking and

start making love. You put up with your mother. You hang
out in libraries.

And stuff like that.

So, obviously that changes you from a behaviour point
of view.

People see you differently, and I understand where they're
coming from, I'm not criticizing. Obviously I can't make
everybody happy: them and me.

But at the same time, I don't give a toss.

O NE MORNING I found my mother standing in the middle of the lettuce patch in the rain talking to a hose pipe.

"You'd be better off going back inside," I said.

"Why?"

"Because it's raining."

"Oh, I can see you coming, you and your tricks," she said.

"All right, fine, it's not raining. It's just water falling. Just look at the state of your slippers."

I walked her back up to the house. She fought me every step of the way, screaming for me to let go, calling me a thug and an ungrateful little brat and saying how I should be ashamed, manhandling a poor woman like her. I thought to myself, One of these days, the neighbours will call the cops, we'll be declared a national disaster and a human rights violation and then we'll be royally screwed.

I pretty much had to carry her, and she weighs a ton.

In her bedroom there was a black dress hanging on the door of the wardrobe.

"Are you going to a funeral?" I said, "Has old man Dupuis finally kicked the bucket?"

"No," she said, "The dress is for me. For when I die. I want to be buried in that dress, it's the only decent one I have."

"What are you on about?" I said, "You've got twenty years in you yet."

Probably thirty, you old hag, I thought to myself.

Since she seemed a bit under the weather, I made her some coffee and put her to bed.

Then I went round to Landremont to ask him to help me fix my ignition.

She died that night.

It's funny, I was so sure she'd be the death of me.

She passed away from something or other I didn't really understand; an attack, I think. Something clean and quick, in any case. I filed her death certificate at the town hall and dealt with everything else, the undertakers and all that.

Everyone came to the funeral. Landremont was completely rat-arsed given that, by free association, funerals always remind him of his poor departed Corinne.

But the drunker he gets, the more dignified he is, so in the circumstances, he fitted right in.

Jojo, Julien and Marco helped me carry the coffin.

Francine lent us her place for the reception, which was mostly just us—and gave us a chance to give Jojo a send-off. Annette and Francine had made beautiful centrepieces and they had even made place cards, writing people's names on leftover sympathy cards.

On the family side, given the hecatomb—a word that contains *tomb* and means everyone is dead—there was only my grandmother, who spent the meal making uncalled-for remarks—*see also: unjustified, unreasonable, unfair, inappropriate*—about the coffin, the flowers, my friends, the meal, such a waste, such a waste! Spending all that money, and for what?

"Give it a rest, Mémé!"

"Oh, you, you're a shiftless layabout. You're no better than that slut of a mother of yours!"

"Yes, Mémé."

"Germain, who's that fat woman sucking the face off the young man in the kitchen?"

"That's Francine, Mémé."

"Has she not noticed he's an Arab?"

"For God's sake, Mémé, please shut up."

Since it was getting to be a pain in the arse, Landremont nipped behind the counter to make her a cocktail. Taste that, Madame Chazes, it's good for what ails you.

"It's very nice," she said, "Would you make us another one?"

I said to Landremont: "Go easy, will you? She's eighty."

"Don't worry. I gave her the kiddie dose."

Not long after that, we tucked my grandmother into Francine's bed and we finally got a bit of peace.

Maître olivier phoned me on Wednesday, for condolence purposes: What a tragedy, Monsieur Chazes, such a wonderful woman! And so young! And so sudden!

"I'm afraid so," I said, "We're just dust in the wind."

"While I'm about it, Monsieur Chazes, I wanted to suggest you might come by my office so that we can discuss the provisions of your late mother's estate."

And it was at this point that he told me that I was going to inherit the house and the land.

"That must be a mistake," I said, "My mother was a tenant."

"No, no," he said, "not at all, she bought it more than twenty years ago and you are her sole heir."

That was not all, he added, she had left something else, but on the phone, well, it would hardly be discreet…

He wanted to enquire about my availability, in order to arrange a convenient time to meet.

"I've got nothing but availability, so every day is convenient," I said.

I'd finished my fixed-term contract at SOPRAF a week before.

I went in on Friday morning. In addition to her house, where I can't really see myself living since I haven't got a single good memory of the place, my mother had left me a fat wad of cash.

For years, she had scrimped and saved for her son—for me, in other words.

It was unbelievable. When I was a kid she treated me like a stray dog under her feet. The minute I said an angry word, *whack*, I'd get a slap faster than a chair in a cop's face. And while all this was going on, she spent every bloody day the Good Lord gave her putting money aside for my old age?!

Go figure.

At the lawyer's office, there was a big envelope with my name on it. It was full of rubbish, a couple of Babygros, a hospital wristband marked *Germain* and a bit of plastic cord that was all purple and shrivelled.

"What the hell is that shit?" I said.

Maître Olivier gave me a funny look.

"Um… I think I remember… obviously I did not pry into your late mother's affairs, but as it happens she told me… so, well, I believe it is a piece of the cord."

"What cord?"

"The umbilical cord. It is a piece of your umbilical cord, I think… so I believe…"

In the envelope there was also a photograph of her as a young girl on a merry-go-round with some guy with pale eyes, and on the back of it she'd written *Me and Germain Despuis, 14th July 1962.*

So this was my old man, then, at the famous carnival a couple of hours before he put a bun in her oven.

Jesus H. Christ on a bike, I thought, so he was called Germain too?

Turns out Margueritte was right all along...

Before I left I said to Maître Olivier:

"So, I was wondering... when someone writes a will and they put in a last wish..."

"Yes? How can I be of service?"

"The person who opens the will, they have to do what it says, don't they?"

"No, no. Not at all. It is entirely a matter of personal judgement. If the deceased includes a wish that is impossible to fulfil, or one that would entail a legal or moral transgression, they are not obliged to blindly abide by his desiderata."

"?..."

"Do you understand?"

"So... you're saying they can't be forced to carry out his last wishes?"

"They cannot be compelled to do so in any circumstance. Why do you ask?"

"No reason, forget about it."

All the same, I was hacked off, on account of the war memorial and Jacques Devallée turning out to be right again as per usual. But as I was thinking this, it occurred to me that for a while now I hadn't been writing my name.

I think maybe, deep down, I don't care any more about being indelible.

THE LAWYER gave me the envelope and shook my hand twice.

I went home with all this crap and dumped it in the middle of the table.

When Annette came round to see me, she said, What's that?

"Keepsakes my mother hung on to," I said.

She picked up the photo and sat next to the window and asked me:

"Is that your mother?"

I said yes.

"How old would she have been?"

"I don't know, but given my age she would have been eighteen. Well, not quite. It was taken the day my father got her pregnant. With me."

"She was really pretty, wasn't she? It's amazing, you'd never have thought it to look at her... So the man in the picture, he's your father?"

I said uh-huh.

"Have you seen the photo before?"

"No, never."

"It must be strange, seeing what he looked like."

I said yeah.

"He looks a hell of a lot older than your mother."

I said, No, not that much really.

He was twelve years older than her, he fucked her at the Bastille Day dance.

Annette is nine years younger than me, I fucked her at the May Day dance.

Maybe my eyes aren't the only thing I get from my father.

Annette cupped my face in both hands and, as if she could read my mind, she said:

"Let me see your eyes."

"Stop…"

"Come on, let me see. You take after him, don't you? You do, honestly, look for yourself. And he was a big man too. But he wasn't as good-looking as you."

"Like hell."

"You're the handsome one, *chéri*."

"Oh, shut up and don't talk rubbish."

"You know how to shut me up, don't you?" She gave me a wink and then kissed me the way only she knows how.

It's weird, but sometimes I think Annette hasn't got a bone in her body. You can hug her as hard as you like and she's soft all the way through.

She's like a duvet, except she's a woman.

Later, she asked me:

"What are you going to do with all these mementos?"

I had no idea. This was one more stupid idea of my mother's, leaving her old tat to me. Out of sheer spite.

Because I knew her like she was my own mother. She knew perfectly well I'm not the kind of guy to go throwing out umbilical cords and photos of my anonymous father—especially when there's only one of them.

Annette said:

"You know what you should do? Put it all in a nice little box, and that's that."

"And what am I supposed to do with the box? Put it on top of the TV?"

"You bury it."

Given that nearly all my relatives were already six feet under, it didn't sound like a stupid idea.

"Or maybe…" Annette said. And she stopped.

"Or maybe what?"

"Maybe you keep it for your own kids… The photo, at least. It would be good for them to have at least one photo of their grandparents."

"Sure, it would be good, if I had any kids."

"…"

"Really?"

Annette's eyes lit up like a Christmas tree. She said:

"Only if you want to, darling. We'll only keep it if you want to. Do you?"

I said, Well, yeah, obviously.

What can you do?

She wound her arms around me and laughed.

She said, My love, my love.

And then: I'm sure it's a girl.
And after that: We'll be happy, you'll see.

I think I can already see.

T HE NEXT DAY, I told Margueritte about my mother. She put her hand on mine and said:

"Your mother? Oh, Germain, I'm so sorry! That's dreadful news."

"Well, you know, me and my mother…"

I didn't say any more, she wouldn't have understood. Margueritte comes from a world where mothers have fibre. I didn't want to tell her all the stuff I've told you, about the screaming matches, disturbing the neighbours, the fucked-up photo albums, the slammed doors, all that shit.

The day I spilled my guts—when she gave me the dictionary—I saw that she was upset for me. She's got enough worries without me adding to them.

When you love people, you hide things from them.

The thing between my mother and me is closed owing to bereavement. There's nothing more to add, best to leave well enough alone.

Margueritte probably thinks I'm sad. But I'm not, and I'm not even ashamed. How could I explain that, sitting with her on this park bench, we've talked more than I ever did with my poor mother—I say "poor" out of respect, not feeling, believe me. And that my mother kicking the bucket doesn't cause me any grief at all? And that I don't even feel grateful about the will and the inheritance, just a bit pissed off that she cared about me but she never bloody bothered to tell me?

I think with kids, it's best to get them to love you while you're still alive. That's how I see things. That's how we see things, Annette and me.

I changed the subject, that was all I could do. I said:

"Would you like to come round for lunch one Sunday if I come and pick you up?"

"To your house?"

"Well, to the caravan. There's a table that seats four, and it's not like you take up much room… And if the weather's nice, we can set up the table outside. You can see my garden."

She laughed and said:

"Why not? It would be a pleasure…"

We talked about the menu, she said she would bring the dessert.

I'll go round and pick her up next Sunday at eleven o'clock sharp.

And then she said:

"In return, I would very much like to invite you to lunch at Les Peupliers, Germain. I do hope you'll come."

"Well, yeah, of course, but I don't really know if I'm allowed," I said.

"Of course you are: the residents are allowed to invite family members one Sunday a month. I'll tell them you're my grandson."

Hearing her say that, I thought we'd adopted each other vice versa which was handy from a feelings standpoint.

"Your grandson? Me? You think they'll believe you?"

"Oh, I think we bear more than a passing resemblance to each other, don't you? Especially as we're both so tall…"

I laughed.

"I suppose we do look a bit alike," I said.

GERMAIN'S READING LIST

ALBERT CAMUS
The Plague / La Peste

JULES SUPERVIELLE
The Child of the High Seas / L'Enfant de la haute mer

ROMAIN GARY
The Promise of Dawn / La Promesse de l'aube

LUIS SEPÚLVEDA
The Old Man Who Read Love Stories /
Un viejo que leía novelas de amor

excerpt from the translation
by Peter Bush, (Souvenir Press 1993)

PUSHKIN PRESS

Pushkin Press was founded in 1997, and publishes novels, essays, memoirs, children's books—everything from timeless classics to the urgent and contemporary.

Our books represent exciting, high-quality writing from around the world: we publish some of the twentieth century's most widely acclaimed, brilliant authors such as Stefan Zweig, Marcel Aymé, Teffi, Antal Szerb, Gaito Gazdanov and Yasushi Inoue, as well as compelling and award-winning contemporary writers, including Andrés Neuman, Edith Pearlman, Eka Kurniawan and Ayelet Gundar-Goshen.

Pushkin Press publishes the world's best stories, to be read and read again. Here are just some of the titles from our long and varied list. To discover more, visit www.pushkinpress.com.

═══

THE SPECTRE OF ALEXANDER WOLF

GAITO GAZDANOV

'A mesmerising work of literature' Antony Beevor

SUMMER BEFORE THE DARK

VOLKER WEIDERMANN

'For such a slim book to convey with such poignancy the extinction of a generation of "Great Europeans" is a triumph' *Sunday Telegraph*

MESSAGES FROM A LOST WORLD

STEFAN ZWEIG

'At a time of monetary crisis and political disorder... Zweig's celebration of the brotherhood of peoples reminds us that there is another way' *The Nation*

BINOCULAR VISION

EDITH PEARLMAN

'A genius of the short story' Mark Lawson, *Guardian*

IN THE BEGINNING WAS THE SEA
TOMÁS GONZÁLEZ

'Smoothly intriguing narrative, with its touches of sinister, Patricia Highsmith-like menace' *Irish Times*

BEWARE OF PITY
STEFAN ZWEIG

'Zweig's fictional masterpiece' *Guardian*

THE ENCOUNTER
PETRU POPESCU

'A book that suggests new ways of looking at the world and our place within it' *Sunday Telegraph*

WAKE UP, SIR!
JONATHAN AMES

'The novel is extremely funny but it is also sad and poignant, and almost incredibly clever' *Guardian*

THE WORLD OF YESTERDAY
STEFAN ZWEIG

'*The World of Yesterday* is one of the greatest memoirs of the twentieth century, as perfect in its evocation of the world Zweig loved, as it is in its portrayal of how that world was destroyed' David Hare

WAKING LIONS
AYELET GUNDAR-GOSHEN

'A literary thriller that is used as a vehicle to explore big moral issues. I loved everything about it' *Daily Mail*

BONITA AVENUE
PETER BUWALDA

'One wild ride: a swirling helix of a family saga… a new writer as toe-curling as early Roth, as roomy as Franzen and as caustic as Houellebecq' *Sunday Telegraph*

JOURNEY BY MOONLIGHT
ANTAL SZERB

'Just divine… makes you imagine the author has had private access to your own soul' Nicholas Lezard, *Guardian*

BEFORE THE FEAST
SAŠA STANIŠIĆ

'Exceptional... cleverly done, and so mesmerising from
the off... thought-provoking and energetic' *Big Issue*

A SIMPLE STORY
LEILA GUERRIERO

'An epic of noble proportions... [Guerriero] is a mistress
of the telling phrase or the revealing detail' *Spectator*

FORTUNES OF FRANCE
ROBERT MERLE

1 *The Brethren*
2 *City of Wisdom and Blood*
3 *Heretic Dawn*

'Swashbuckling historical fiction' *Guardian*

TRAVELLER OF THE CENTURY
ANDRÉS NEUMAN

'A beautiful, accomplished novel: as ambitious as it is generous,
as moving as it is smart' Juan Gabriel Vásquez, *Guardian*

ONE NIGHT, MARKOVITCH
AYELET GUNDAR-GOSHEN

'Wry, ironically tinged and poignant... this is a fable
for the twenty-first century' *Sunday Telegraph*

KARATE CHOP & MINNA NEEDS REHEARSAL SPACE
DORTHE NORS

'Unique in form and effect... Nors has found a novel
way of getting into the human heart' *Guardian*

RED LOVE: THE STORY OF AN EAST GERMAN
FAMILY
MAXIM LEO

'Beautiful and supremely touching... an unbearably poignant
description of a world that no longer exists' *Sunday Telegraph*

SONG FOR AN APPROACHING STORM
PETER FRÖBERG IDLING

'Beautifully evocative... a must-read novel' *Daily Mail*